BOOK TWENTY-NINE

The seaweed draped across her bed that morning warned Norah that the ghost of Jenny Swift was real. No human being could have entered without disturbing the locks of the doors and windows.

But if the ghost was real, then so was the curse. And unless Barnabas could shield her, Norah was doomed to die under the blacksnake whip of the phantom pirate queen!

Hermes Press

Published by Hermes Press, an imprint of
Herman and Geer Communications, Inc.

Daniel Herman, Publisher
Troy Musguire, Production Manager
Eileen Sabrina Herman, Managing Editor
Alissa Fisher, Graphic Design
Kandice Hartner, Senior Editor

2100 Wilmington Road
Neshannock, Pennsylvania 16105
(724) 652-0511
www.HermesPress.com; info@hermespress.com

Book design by Eileen Sabrina Herman
First printing, 2022

LCCN applied for: 10 9 8 7 6 5 4 3 2 1 0
ISBN: 978-1-61345-255-4
OCR and text editing by H + G Media and Eileen Sabrina Herman
Proof reading by Eileen Sabrina Herman and Shah Saleem

From Dan, Sabrina, and Jacob in memory of Al DeVivo

Acknowledgments: This book would not be possible without the help and encouragement of Jim Pierson and Curtis Holdings

Barnabas, Quentin and the Sea Ghost
by Marilyn Ross

CONTENTS

CHAPTER 1

Switching the car radio on, Norah Bliss learned that the weather bureau had issued a warning of a severe coastal storm. Shipping had been advised to seek shelter for the next dozen hours. She glanced anxiously at her father, who was sitting in the front seat beside her.

"Do you suppose we'll manage to get to Collinsport before the storm breaks?" she asked. She was an attractive girl in her early twenties with long blonde hair which she wore straight down around her shoulders.

Claude Bliss, prematurely gray and spare of frame, smiled, the lines around his eyes crinkling. "I doubt if the storm will be that bad on shore," he said. "It's mostly a warning for mariners."

"I hope you're right," she said and gave her attention to the wheel again. The traffic was busy, since they were still in the suburban area of Boston.

"We shouldn't be too much delayed at Portsmouth," her father said. "And that's the only stop we'll be making. With luck we'll be there well before dark."

"I'm glad of that," Norah said. Since she'd taken over as her father's secretary she'd come to know his moods. Just now he was too busy thinking about the major project ahead to be concerned with the weather of the day.

Claude Bliss Underwater Explorations, Inc. was recognized as the most successful salvage company in the United States. Her father, once a diver himself, had formed the organization to explore the coastal waters of North America and the West Indies, salvaging wrecked ships, ancient and modern, and recovering their treasure. It had made him wealthy but he'd also become obsessed with the adventure of it. The attention he gave to his work made him sometimes maddeningly unaware of daily living problems.

Just now they were heading for the small Maine town of Collinsport near Bar Harbor. They would be remaining there for the summer while her father directed an attempt to locate and recover the treasure from a pirate ship lost in Collinsport Cove more than two hundred years ago. The expedition had been widely publicized, since a number of others had tried to recover the enormous treasure without success, and because her father was using a new kind of bathysphere which he had personally designed. It was to be put in practical use for the first time at Collinsport.

Glancing from the traffic to the dark clouds forming overhead, Norah said, "I have an idea the storm is moving in on us sooner than predicted."

"Perhaps," her father said absently, his blank expression warning her his thoughts were still miles away.

"We have to drive outside the town of Collinsport, don't we?"

He nodded. "Yes. We take the shore road to the Collinwood estate."

"That means we'll be on an isolated, exposed road at the very end of our journey."

"I'm sure it isn't as remote as all that," her father said.

She sighed. "I wouldn't mind if we were arriving before dark. But a strange road in a bad storm frightens me."

He gave her a reassuring glance. "I'm certain we'll manage very well."

"You really aren't worrying about it at all," Norah reproved him. "Or even thinking about it, for that matter."

"Sorry," he said. "I'm reviewing in my mind some of the matters I have to discuss with Commander Grayson."

Norah uttered a tiny groan as she shot ahead of a truck in the other lane. "I knew your mind was somewhere else!"

"We'll be arriving at the Portsmouth Naval Base soon," Claude Bliss said, "and I want to have everything arranged in my mind. That way we lose less time."

"Is it absolutely necessary that we stop there?"

"I'm afraid so. They've some last minute work to do on the bathysphere before towing it to Collinsport. They want to discuss a few changes in design with me."

"That could take hours!"

"No. The changes aren't that important," her father said. "Since we'll be arriving there at lunch time, the best plan might be to combine the luncheon with our business discussion."

Norah looked bleak. "I can picture it going on for hours. You and Commander Grayson always reminisce when you're together."

Claude Bliss looked apologetic. "During the Korean War we were in the service together."

"I know all about it," she said despairingly. "And I'll be bound to hear it again during lunch."

"It can't be all that boring for you!"

"It isn't. But I'll grudge every minute knowing we have a long drive and the storm ahead."

Her father sighed. "I'll make it as quick as I can."

"We've been through this before," she said. "It will take longer than you expect"

Bliss gave his daughter a troubled glance. "You don't sound very happy."

"I suppose I'm not."

"I mean, I'm beginning to think you're not happy working with me. Perhaps it has been a mistake."

She glanced from the wheel a moment to give her father a shocked look. "I thrive on the adventure of this work. You must know that."

Her father looked unconvinced. "Sometimes I worry that it's merely a matter of too much dedication to me. When your mother died you became the center of my life, aside from my work. Perhaps I have overdone the fond father bit."

Now Norah was beginning to feel guilty. "Nonsense," she said. "I elected to work with you because I like underwater exploration."

"But it confines you to isolated locations and few companions."

"I like the atmosphere. It's good to get away from the cities."

"But you're not meeting any eligible young men," her father said. "Wouldn't you be better off working in some large organization in New York or some other city where you'd meet plenty of young men?"

She gave him a wry, amused glance. "Now you're sounding like a matchmaker. You don't have to worry. You have only one daughter to marry off and she has lots of time yet."

"I wonder."

"I know," she said firmly.

"I want you to live a life of your own," her father said. "This way you seem so tied to me."

She had reached the toll station on the New Hampshire

Turnpike and now she slowed down to drop a quarter into the automatic lane toll slot. "Because I'm worried about getting to Collinsport before the storm breaks, you think I'm dissatisfied with my entire life," she said with amused irony as she accelerated again. "Besides, I've had several chances to get married. Dick Owens for one."

"You left Dick alone for a summer to go to Jamaica with me," her father said. "And by the time you returned he was engaged to someone else."

"I knew what was happening."

"Then why didn't you leave me and go back to him?"

She smiled ruefully. "For the simplest of reasons. I didn't want to. We wrote to each other regularly and gradually we realized that we wouldn't manage a good marriage."

Her father shook his head. "I don't think you'd have been so realistic if your working for me hadn't parted you two."

"In that case the parting was a blessing," she told him. "I've seen too many of my friends make hasty, unwise marriages. I can wait for the right man."

"I wonder if you'll recognize him," he said with a thin smile.

She laughed lightly. "I'm sure I will."

"We'll see. But if ever you feel you want to get away from me and my work, don't hesitate."

"I won't."

"That must be a promise," he said seriously.

She sighed as they drove along. "All this because I mentioned I didn't want to be kept at Portsmouth too long!"

"Sorry."

She gave him another glance. "You won't stay any longer than you need to, will you? We are going to be caught at night in the storm if you do."

"I'll keep it in mind."

"I hope so. When will the rest of the crew arrive and where are they staying?"

"They will arrive on the tug that tows the bathysphere from Portsmouth," Claude Bliss said. "And some of them will live aboard it and a scow we're having rigged out as a houseboat. The balance will live in a cottage on the grounds of Collinwood."

"Then if you give an okay on the bathysphere today, they'll be arriving very shortly to begin the work."

"In another week at the latest, I hope."

At the entrance of the Navy Shipyard, a guard at the gate halted them for credentials.

"I'm Claude Bliss. I have an appointment with Commander Grayson."

The young man nodded. "Commander Grayson is expecting you. You'll find him at the Officers' Dining Hall. Do you know where it is?"

Norah smiled. "Yes. I'm afraid we've been here before."

"Very well. Miss," the young man said and saluted as they moved on.

"I like these young navy men," she told her father as they drove toward the frame structure which housed the Officers' Dining Hall. "They're so polite."

Commander Grayson was waiting to greet them in the lobby of the dining hall. He was a broad man of medium height with a square, florid face and iron gray hair. Heavy eyebrows, still surprisingly black, crowned eyes of gray which held a twinkle in them.

"Welcome to the base, both of you," he said warmly, shaking hands.

He escorted them to a white-clothed table in a quiet area of the big dining room and after they had ordered he joked in the usual manner with her father.

"You're really going to strike it rich this time, Claude," the Commander teased. "Save me some pieces of eight."

Her father frowned. "The most important thing is whether you've got the diving bell ready or not. Everything depends on that bathysphere."

The Commander nodded. "I realize that. There are just a few items we'll go over after luncheon before sending it out."

Bliss gave Norah a knowing smile. "Norah predicted we'd waste a lot of time talking at lunch and then get away to a late start. We're driving on to Collinsport tonight."

The florid face of the Commander registered amusement. "I'm afraid you know us too well, Miss Norah."

"At least I won't be surprised if it does happen," she said with a small smile of her own. "It's not that I don't find your stories fascinating. I simply hate the idea of driving in a storm."

She realized later she'd made a bad error in calling their yarns fascinating, for as soon as luncheon was served her father and the Commander began exchanging anecdotes.

Commander Grayson began telling of his work as a diver in salvaging a four-thousand-ton freighter off the coast of Virginia. "She lay sixty-five feet down. And though she had a blanket of marine organisms, she really looked like a sunken ship. Many of them don't. But she taught me a lot about the peril of wrecks. Many of her surfaces were adorned with a nasty little variety of razor-edged incisor clam. We had to watch for them."

Her father nodded. "I've hit on them when I've been skin

diving. Brush your body against them and you get a bad cut. And underwater cuts are usually painless. The sea knows no difference between blood and water."

"Exactly," the Commander agreed. "The wood of this wreck had almost crumbled away, but the ironwork had barely rusted. And although the water around it was clear, the holds were full of yellowish water, much colder than the sea water outside. I learned a lot working on her. I made my way to the engine room and each deck removed more light, shut another door between us and the sun and air. I moved on down to the engine room and it was almost completely dark."

Norah shivered. "Most of my diving has been where the water is fairly shallow and the sun penetrates all the way."

The Commander chuckled. "I found treasures down there. I brought up electric-light bulbs that still worked and a glass bejeweled with corals." He winked at her father. "You will have to do much better with your pirate treasure ship."

"I'm sure we will," her father said.

"You're one of the few outfits that have any success," Commander Grayson said. "Whenever I read about companies raising capital to outfit treasure hunting expeditions to the ocean's bottom, I have the impression more money will be raised on the surface than ever below the water."

Norah smiled at him. "You must have faith in my father or you wouldn't have worked on the bathysphere as you have."

"I do," he said seriously. "And this diving bell should help you in working on that wreck in Collinsport Cove. Your men can use it as an underwater headquarters."

Claude Bliss sighed. "It may not be so easy. Others have failed before us. But I have faith. Yet the wreck occurred centuries ago and the water is deeper than one would expect. The important thing will be to first find out the exact location of the sunken hull."

"It may have shifted some over the years," the Commander agreed.

Their conversation went on through the luncheon and then they went out to the docks to inspect the diving bell. It was a steel ball nearly eight feet in diameter. On either side of the ball were electric motors which would drive propellers to move it around under water. The ball itself was molded of three-and-a-half inch thick steel with two heavy steel hatches.

"It's terribly impressive," Norah confessed.

Commander Grayson nodded. "We'll have a look inside."

They descended into the diving bell where two technicians were working on switches. Norah gazed around at the formidable maze of controls with awe, while her father discussed the indicators, gauges and other instruments. She gathered that three men could live in the bathysphere for twenty-four hours.

At last the check on the diving bell was completed, and Commander Grayson promised to have the equipment towed to Collinsport within the week. Norah and her father hurried back to their car, but by the time they reached the expressway the dark clouds were really ominous and it was starting to rain.

Norah said, "I'm afraid we stayed too long. The storm has begun in earnest."

Her father was still lost in speculation about his beloved diving bell. Ignoring her comment, he told her, "Grayson has done a marvelous job on the bathysphere. If he gets it to us as soon as he promised, we'll avoid any delays in starting the search for the treasure."

"You didn't hear a thing I said, did you?"

He showed mild surprise. "Did I miss something?"

She gestured at the rain-splattered windshield. "You did. The change in the weather."

"It does look nasty."

"It will be worse before we get another hundred miles," she worried. "You and Commander Grayson and all your talk!"

"You said you found it interesting."

"I did. But now we're going to pay for it."

"Just drive carefully," her father said. "It doesn't matter if we're a little late."

"Are the Collins family so interested in the treasure hunt they want us to live with them?" she asked.

"Yes," her father said. "Roger Collins thinks the publicity from our project has done the town good already. There have been a lot of inquiries from prospective tourists."

"What sort of place is this Collinwood?"

"A fine old mansion," her father said. "I spent a night there when I first went down to see about salvaging *The Jenny Swift*. They were extremely kind to me and it was then they invited us to stay with them while we're searching for a pirate treasure ship."

"Won't we be imposing on them?"

"Their house has forty rooms," her father said. "They'll hardly know we're around. And you should have company. There are two young people in the house. The younger is a boy named David. His cousin Carolyn is in her late teens."

"It will be nice to have some young people around," she said.

"I feel the same way," her father agreed.

"The Collins family must be wealthy."

"They have had a successful fish-packing business for years," Bliss explained. "In the beginning they sent out salted fish, but now they can do a great deal of it."

"They must have grown up with the story of the shipwreck of *The Jenny Swift*," she suggested.

"No question about that. Everyone in the area knows about the pirate ship and how it was lost. In fact, one of the local wealthy people organized his own expedition to find the treasure."

"What happened?"

"They didn't locate *The Jenny Swift* and ran out of working capital. It was just one of many unsuccessful attempts."

"And you think we have a chance to succeed?"

"Yes. We have new and superior equipment," her father said. "None of the other groups had that advantage."

The late afternoon had become so dark she was forced to turn on the headlights. The rain grew heavier and a strong wind had risen, which occasionally actually swayed the car as they drove along. Her misgivings grew and she fervently wished they had gotten away from Portsmouth earlier.

"I hate to arrive at a strange house on a stormy night," she worried. "The Collins family will be disgusted with us from the minute we get there."

"They can hardly blame the weather on us," her father said.

"They can blame us, and rightly, for not timing our arrival better," she told him.

With the headlights and the windshield wipers both going at full power she still had difficulty seeing the road ahead. Because of this, she was forced to reduce the speed of the car greatly.

Her father sat forward a little, staring at the road. "It is bad, isn't it?"

"And we have miles to go yet!"

The storm broke with full fury by the time they left the turnpike to take the two-lane winding highway which led to Ellsworth and on to Collinsport. She was beginning to get really weary but she didn't like to ask her father to take a turn at the wheel since she knew he also must be exhausted. He'd worked very hard before they left.

"Are you familiar with this road?" she asked him.

"I've only been over it once," Claude Bliss admitted. "But I know that when we reach the coast we take a turnoff to the right. It leads directly to Collinwood."

"It might be better for us to drive into the village and register at the hotel for the night," she suggested.

"No, I think not," her father said. "The Collins family are expecting us. They might be disappointed."

She frowned, her eyes still on the road ahead. The headlights' glare on the dark wet road made driving twice as difficult as it normally would be. "I only hope I don't miss it."

"I'll watch for the sign," he promised.

By this time the storm was raging wildly. The rain hit the windshield with such gusts that every so often Norah's view was completely blocked.

"I feel like giving up," she complained.

"We can't be more than a mile or so from the main house," her father said. "It's perched on a cliff facing the bay. And there are cliffs all along the left side of this road. So watch out!"

"Thanks for telling me," she said with some sarcasm. "It's all I need to know in order to relax completely."

"Sorry," her father said. "The road is set in from the cliff's edge, for the most part."

"I should hope so."

All at once her annoyance became just plain fear. Up to this point she'd only been upset that they'd gotten such a late start for their journey on this stormy evening. But this new road was narrower than the other one and more twisting. She was having difficulty negotiating the sharp curves and felt that an error could cost them their lives.

She knew that somewhere to the left in the darkness lay the cliff's edge and disaster to anyone who drove too close to it. This alone would have made her tense and afraid, but there was something else. . . .

She had the feeling that they were heading into some evil, some dark fate which they could not comprehend. Suddenly she wished that she had tried to persuade her father against this treasure hunt. *The Jenny Swift* was supposed to be cursed. Disaster had been predicted for anyone attempting to rob the sunken vessel of her treasure. And most of those who had attempted to salvage the riches had been struck down in one fashion or another.

Were they to be the next victims? She didn't want to think about it and yet she had the feeling there was some mystery about Collinwood to which they were heading. Her father hadn't told her much about the old mansion but she was sure she'd read about it when doing some research into the history of the Maine coast.

They came to a sharp turn and she almost didn't manage it. "The road and storm are both getting worse," she told her father.

"Shouldn't you pull over to one side of the road and rest a while?" her father inquired anxiously.

"No use now. We'll do better to push on and try and make it."

"It seems very bad," he said.

"It is," she hastily agreed, swinging into another of those sharp curves.

But this time she didn't swing quite sharply enough.

"Watch out!" she screamed as the car slid into the deep ditch. She fought to control the wheel, knowing it was too late. Finally the car came to a rest, its headlights pointing almost straight up. She switched off the motor and moaned. "Now we're really in trouble."

"Better in the ditch than over the cliff."

"I could have done without either," she told him with a hint of anger.

Her father looked forlorn. "I don't suppose we can get out on our own power?"

"It just isn't possible," she worried. "The ground here is soft and clay-like. We'll only dig in deeper if we try."

"Then what?"

She shrugged. "I'll have to go out in the storm and see if I can get any idea of where Collinwood is located. It may be close to us."

"It can't be too far away," her father agreed. "Let me get out with you."

She tried to dissuade him, but he wouldn't hear of it. He slid across the seat and got out of the wrecked auto with her. The rain beat in their faces as they clambered up to the surface of the road. Reaching it, her father ran a hand through his dripping, windblown hair and peered into the blackness of the night. "I can't see any lights of Collinwood," he finally admitted.

She walked back a few steps, trying for a different angle, then came hurrying to rejoin him. "We're in luck," she told him. "Another car is coming along the road behind us. It should be here in a minute or two."

"We must flag it down," her father said.

"They'll see our headlights pointing skyward and know something is wrong," she predicted.

"Just the same, they must be halted. I'll get a flashlight from the car to signal them." And he went down over the bank to carry out the errand.

She watched him go, sure that he'd get back too late, and moved to the middle of the road as the headlights of the other car came into view. She waved wildly to halt it. As it slowed down she gasped in dismay. The dark vehicle resembled a hearse!

CHAPTER 2

The car lights came blindingly close and then the door opposite the driver's side opened and a tall man in a caped coat got out and came to her through the pouring rain. He had dark brown hair and a handsome gaunt face with piercing eyes. Halting in front of her, he said, "I see you've had some trouble."

"Yes," she said apologetically. "I couldn't see and ran straight into the ditch."

"That's easy to do on this road and on such a night," he said.

"Are we close to Collinwood?"

He nodded. "Yes, quite. In fact I'm on my way there now. I'm Barnabas Collins and I'm going on a little further to what we call the old house."

She managed a smile. "How do you do, Mr. Collins? I'm Norah Bliss. My father and I are going to be staying at Collinwood while we search for a sunken treasure off the coast."

"Ah, yes. Miss Bliss," Barnabas Collins said. "I've heard about your project. Most interesting." He glanced skyward and then smiled grimly at her. "I don't suppose we can stand here in the rain exchanging pleasantries much longer. Your car seems in pretty bad shape. The best plan would be to let it remain there until morning and have one of the village garages send out a tow truck to get it out then."

"You're right," she agreed. "We're getting drenched here." And seeing her father come clambering up the embankment with the flashlight, she said, "Here is my father."

Norah explained the situation quickly, and while her father went back to turn off the headlights and get a couple of overnight bags, Barnabas walked Norah to his car. At least, she supposed it could be called that. It seemed a mixture of hearse and station wagon.

Barnabas told her, "My servant, Willie Loomis, is driving. I'll have him move to the rear of the wagon so you and your father can sit up front with me."

"Will that be terribly inconvenient for you?"

"Not at all," he said. "I'll enjoy taking a spell at the wheel for the last few minutes of the drive. I know the road."

"It certainly is a blessing for us that you came along," she said.

"Happy to be of help," Barnabas assured her. On reaching the vehicle he went to the driver's side and gave some curt instructions to a rather loutish looking young man, who nodded and quickly stepped out into the rain. He gave Norah an interested glance and then went back to meet her father and get the bags.

When she was comfortably installed in the warm front seat next to Barnabas, who was now behind the wheel, she smiled and said, "I'm drenched. I hope you didn't get too wet."

"No. I have my cape. It's excellent for this bad weather," Barnabas said. Peering through the rain-splattered windshield, he added, "I see Willie and your father returning now."

A moment later Claude Bliss got into the cab and sat on the other side of her. "Comfortable in here," he said. "But I'm soaked to the skin from the storm."

"It is terrible," she agreed. At the same time Willie Loomis had gotten into the rear of the wagon with the bags. The rear doors slammed and Barnabas drove on.

Barnabas said pleasantly, "I hope this bad start doesn't tarn you against the area. It can be very nice."

"I'm positive of it," she said.

"We are much indebted to you, Mr. Collins. Would you be a brother to Elizabeth and Roger Collins?" Bliss asked.

"No, a cousin. I have spent much of my time abroad and traveling. But I have a sentimental feeling for Collinwood and return every so often."

Norah said, "You mentioned living in what you termed the old house."

"Yes," Barnabas Collins said in his cultured British voice. "That is what the first Collinwood is called these days. The property was left to me to use."

"How interesting!" she said. "And do your wife and children join you here for the summer?"

The handsome man glanced at her with a melancholy smile. "I regret to say I have neither a wife nor children, Miss Bliss. I live a bachelor existence, but my servant Willie takes care of the household duties very well."

"Interesting," her father said. "But since you travel a lot, no doubt you find it convenient to be unattached."

"Convenient, yes," Barnabas said as they drove on through the wet night. "But it can be lonesome at times. One always has certain regrets."

"True," her father agreed. "No matter what the choice."

Barnabas gave them a friendly glance. "You are famous, Mr. Bliss, and I'm happy you've come to have a try at locating the sunken treasure. I wish you luck."

"It should prove an interesting project," Claude Bliss said. "We have a lot of new equipment to use."

"To simplify things, I suppose?"

"Just so," her father agreed. "Though I must say we've not gotten off to a very happy start."

"I doubt if your car is harmed much," Barnabas Collins said. "And it will be a fairly easy matter to get it towed out in the morning."

Norah studied the handsome profile of the man at the wheel with deep interest. It was hard to judge his age, though she guessed he must be in his thirties. He had a classic, melancholy face.

She said, "You'll be around to watch the salvaging operations?"

"I should be," he agreed politely.

"Your family have lived at Collinwood for centuries, haven't they?" she said.

Barnabas nodded. "Yes."

"Was a Collins living here when *The Jenny Swift* was wrecked?" Norah's father asked.

"I'm not positive about that," Barnabas said. "But if not, certainly very shortly afterward." He indicated ahead. "If you look now you'll see the lights of Collinwood."

She strained her eyes to peer through the rain and darkness and did see lighted windows to the right "We're almost there!"

"Actually driving up the front roadway."

"This has been most opportune for us," Claude Bliss told the handsome stranger. "We shall not forget it, sir."

"I was happy to be of service," Barnabas said as he brought the wagon to a halt.

"Will you be stopping at Collinwood?" Norah asked.

"No," Barnabas said. "My man will put your bags on the steps and then we'll drive on to the other house. It's behind this main house and not far from here."

She said, "I do hope we'll see you often."

His eyes met hers. "I promise you that you will."

At Barnabas' request, Loomis carried their bags to the entrance of Collinwood, despite the protests of Norah and her father that it was unnecessary. Barnabas stood for a moment in the downpour, saying goodnight, before getting back in the vehicle. As Norah watched the long black wagon drive off, she received a kind of jolt. Among the things loaded in its back, she was certain she'd noticed a long gray coffin!

She made no mention of it to her father. Surely she was wrong; she'd mistaken something else for a casket. And even if she were right it was not the proper time to discuss it. With a vague sense of uneasiness she turned to the lighted entrance where her father stood with the bags, having already rung the bell.

A moment later a buxom elderly woman opened the door. Her father said, "Mr. Bliss and his daughter. We're late because our car went into the ditch."

"Of course, Mr. Bliss," the woman said. "Mrs. Stoddard and Mr. Collins have been expecting you. Come straight in and I'll have your bags looked after."

The housekeeper ushered them into an elegantly furnished living room, where a log fire burned in a large stone fireplace. A stem, middle-aged man advanced down the length of the room to greet them. The glow of the crystal chandelier revealed him as balding.

"Mr. Bliss!" he said, shaking hands heartily with her father. "We'd decided that you wouldn't be attempting to complete your journey tonight."

"We shouldn't have," her father admitted. "But I felt we could. As a result our car is in the ditch near here."

"No matter," Roger Collins said. "Just so long as you're not injured, either of you." He tamed to Norah. "This is a great pleasure, Miss Bliss. I am Roger Collins."

She shook hands with him. "My father has spoken of you and Mrs. Stoddard so often lately. And how kind of you to invite us to live here for awhile."

"We've looked forward to it," Roger Collins assured her. He was friendly enough, Norah decided, despite his austere appearance.

"What a wonderful old mansion!" she exclaimed, taking in the rich antiques, the walnut paneled walls and the fine paintings hung around the room.

"We're proud of it," Roger said.

Just then an attractive dark-haired matron joined them.

Norah knew at once this had to be Elizabeth Stoddard. Within a few minutes more David, Roger's shy eleven-year-old son, and Carolyn, who was Elizabeth's pretty teenaged daughter, came to join the group.

"I'm having Mrs. Benson prepare a late meal for you and your father," Elizabeth promised. "It will be ready shortly and perhaps it would be best to serve it in your rooms. You'll want to rest."

"That's too much trouble!" Norah's father protested.

"Nonsense," was Roger Collins' comment. "Elizabeth has plenty of help. It presents no problem."

They were gathered by the fireplace, with the men standing and Norah and the other women of the group seated. Norah's father said, "I must say we are greatly indebted to your cousin, Barnabas Collins, for his kindness to us."

It was as if an electric shock had gone through the room. All except David looked startled. There was a brief silence, then Roger Collins cleared his throat and asked, "Am I to understand that you've met Barnabas?"

"Why, yes," Norah's father said. "It was he who came to our assistance when we ditched the car. He just left us off here at the door. Extremely kind of him."

Elizabeth Stoddard had turned slightly pale. "So Barnabas has come back," she said with a meaningful glance at her brother.

"So it would seem," Roger Collins said with a frown.

Norah was curious about the strong reaction they'd all shown to the news. "Didn't you expect him?"

Roger Collins looked grim. "We never really know when Barnabas will arrive. He rarely gives us a warning of his comings or goings."

"I understand he lives in the original Collinwood."

Elizabeth Stoddard sighed. "Yes. For years we have discussed tearing it down, since it is lived in so little. But Barnabas has always been very upset at the idea. In a sense it is his property."

Claude Bliss said, "I gather from his conversation that he travels a great deal."

"He does," Roger said dryly. "I have often wondered why he comes back here."

Carolyn, Elizabeth's lovely daughter, now spoke up impulsively. "But Barnabas loves this place. All of it! He has often told me so." She smiled at Norah. "Don't you think he's very nice, Miss Bliss?"

"He is," she agreed warmly.

"Well, enough of Barnabas," Roger Collins said with a hint of sourness in his tone. "I'm sure you both must be very weary from your journey. You'll want to go to your rooms and rest and have some food."

Norah's father said, "It sounds extremely attractive to me."

"And to me," Norah echoed.

"Excellent," Roger Collins said with a smile which could have been forced. "Dr. Julia Hoffman and her associate, Professor Stokes, will be here tomorrow night to discuss the business details of the project. They are more than willing to assist in sponsoring it."

"That is good news," her father said. "The bathysphere is ready to be towed here and we can begin work at once."

"No need to worry about it until you are settled in," Roger Collins told him. "Now I understand by what you said that your car is ditched not any further than a mile or two from here."

"Yes," Norah's father said.

"If you'll leave me the keys," Roger suggested, "I'll call one of our trucks at the factory and have them get you out. No need to depend on a service station."

"That is truly generous of you." Her father rummaged in his coat pocket and produced the keys after a moment. He passed them to Roger.

Elizabeth was on her feet. "I'll take Mr. Bliss to his room and you show Norah to hers, Carolyn. She's to have the room down the hall from you on the second floor."

Carolyn got up with a smile. "I'll be glad to." She turned to Norah. "Come along." And she led her out of the big living room and up the wide, carpeted stairway.

On the dimly lighted stairway, she said, "You must have noticed how strangely they behaved about your mention of Barnabas."

Somewhat embarrassed, Norah ventured, "They did seem startled."

"They're old-fashioned and stuffy," Carolyn said, frowning. "I'm personally very fond of Barnabas and think he is a fine gentleman. I wanted you to know."

Norah, who had already inferred that opinion was widely divided about this British cousin, said, "I was impressed by him during our short meeting."

"He keeps to himself a lot when he's here. It's likely you'll only see him after dusk. But pay no attention to any mean remarks you may hear about him."

Norah, puzzled, said merely, "I'll remember that." They came to the open door of a lighted bedroom and as Carolyn showed her into it she saw her bag on the bed. Everything was handled very efficiently at Collinwood, it seemed.

Carolyn glanced around and made sure that the room was in order. "I hope you'll find everything you need here. Otherwise let me know."

"Thank you," Norah said, taking in the big room with its blue and white decor and white drapes. "It's lovely."

"We have a large house," Carolyn said. "And since we're rather isolated, it is nice to have company. And don't let David bother you. He's all excited about the treasure hunt; the first chance he gets he'll ply you with a lot of questions."

She laughed. "I won't mind. He seems like a nice boy."

"He is, though he can be full of pranks when he likes," Carolyn sighed. "Mrs. Benson will be sending up your snack in a short time. Goodnight."

"Goodnight."

It was a pleasant ending, Norah thought, to a difficult night. Already she was feeling weary and anxious to get to bed. While she waited for the food to arrive she began unpacking. Fortunately all she needed for overnight had been packed in the small bag which she'd used along the journey from New York.

She'd scarcely finished unpacking when there was a knock on the door. She opened it and a stout, youthful maid came in with a tray. The girl nodded to her in a polite, friendly manner and said, "I'm Lucy. Mrs. Benson sent this up. Mind the plate. It's hot." And she sat it on the table by the window.

"Thank you, Lucy. Will you be back for the tray?"

"No," the maid said. "Just leave it on the table and I'll get it when I clean in the morning. Is there anything else?"

"Not that I can think of," Norah said, sitting at the table and uncovering the plate to discover an excellent Welsh rarebit. "This looks delicious," she exclaimed.

Lucy looked complacent. "Yes, Miss. Cook does well with most foods. Are you the lady who came to find the sunken treasure?"

"My father is heading the expedition."

Lucy looked interested. "My old Dad told me about *The Jenny Swift* when I was just a little tike. He claimed the ship was cursed. And everyone who tried to get the treasure has been cursed as well. Something always happens to them. Aren't you afraid, miss?"

She shook her head. "No. Hunting for sunken treasure and exploring the wrecks of vessels under the ocean are nothing new to us."

"But you know there are more ghosts at Collinwood than almost anywhere else," the maid said solemnly.

Norah raised her eyebrows. "What gives you that idea?"

"Known fact, miss. Why, the Bangor Star had a story about this old house in the Sunday section a couple of years ago. That was when I first came to work here and I tell you it made my flesh fair creep."

"They ran a story about ghosts at Collinwood?"

"Indeed, they did, miss. They told about how long ago the place was put under a curse by a she-devil from the West Indies by the name of Angelique. It was her who out of jealousy turned Barnabas Collins into a vampire. Made him one of the living dead."

Norah paused over her food to stare at the girl. "Did you say that Barnabas Collins had been turned into a vampire?"

"Yes, miss. That was the beginning. Then there were others. Quentin, who would change into a wolf man when the moon was full. And too many more to mention. I can tell you, none of the girls working here will leave the house at night unless their boyfriends come to get them. A lot of queer things have happened around here."

Norah listened with some amazement. She said, "But I met Barnabas Collins tonight and he was very nice."

Lucy stared at her. In a low, hushed voice, she said, "You mean he has come back?"

"Yes."

"He and that crazy Willie Loomis who drives that hearse they travel in?"

"It does look something like a hearse," Norah admitted. "But I suppose it's actually a station wagon."

"I don't care what it is, it sure looks scary to me," Lucy said. "The Barnabas Collins you met is a descendant of the one I was talking about. But he looks like the first Barnabas. There's a picture of the one who became a vampire in the hallway and it's the spitting image of this Barnabas."

"I must look at it."

"Do that," Lucy said. "And mind yourself around this other Barnabas as well. He hasn't got a very good reputation."

"I'm surprised you say that."

"Mr. Roger and Mrs. Stoddard know about him," Lucy said grimly. "They've had their time protecting the Collins family name with him around. There's a story told that he has only two weaknesses, walking alone in cemeteries at night and attacking pretty girls. And they say if he isn't busy with one he's doing the other."

She frowned. "But that's a dreadful way to talk about anyone. Especially anyone as pleasant as Barnabas Collins. Carolyn warned me I'd be hearing gossip about him and told me not to believe it."

The stout girl looked uneasy. "I didn't mean to say anything out of turn, miss."

"Well, it sounded much like it."

"I was only trying to warn you, miss. Funny things have gone on here. And once or twice I've known guests in this house to have experiences with ghosts. And even worse!"

A sudden gust of wind swept the window with rain. Norah grimaced and looked out into the dark, stormy night. "I must say you're giving me a frightening picture of Collin wood, Lucy."

"Seems to me you should know."

"From what you tell me ghosts are fairly toppling over one another here," Norah said with a wry smile.

"It's not anything to joke about, miss," the maid assured her. "Dad told me about walking along the cliffs and meeting the woman pirate, Jenny Swift, himself. Fair made my blood run cold to hear him describe her reaching out and smiling at him and her with the wet seaweed from the ocean where she came from hanging from her hair down to her shoulders."

"You think he really saw a ghost?"

"He wouldn't lie, miss," was the girl's earnest reply. "Maybe you don't know the story about the wreck. But according to what I've heard, there was an uprising among the crew. They wanted to desert before *The Jenny Swift* sank, but she wouldn't let them. And when one of the masts fell it crushed all the side of her face. So her ghost has one eye that droops from its socket on her broken face. Looks horrible!"

"I don't think I want to hear anymore about her," Norah said. She wasn't superstitious but the combination of the stormy night in this lonely place and the maid's weird stories had set her nerves on edge. She had read one rather short description of Jenny Swift's infamous career, but the account of the wreck and the mutilation of her face was something new.

"Sorry if I bothered you," Lucy said, turning away.

"Oh, look. I didn't mean to hurt your feelings. It's just that— well, on a night like this, everything seems so real."

"It is, miss," the stout girl said solemnly. "You don't have to look any further than Carson Blythe to find out what the curse of *The Jenny Swift* can do!"

"Carson Blythe," Norah repeated. "The name seems familiar."

"It should. He lives just along the cliffs from here. You can see his big house. It's all glass and peaked roofs and built on the face of the cliff itself."

"Modern?"

"Very," the maid agreed. "Well, Mr. Blythe has all kinds of money. But he wasn't satisfied. He went to a year of trouble and expense to try and get the treasure from that sunken pirate ship."

"I know now," Norah said. "And a storm wrecked all his equipment and he gave up."

"That wasn't the worst."

"No?"

"No. Jenny's ghost came to haunt his house. She gave him no rest. They say she appeared almost every night. And it was Mrs. Blythe who was upset the worst about it. It gave her a kind of breakdown. And the upshot of it was she threw herself from the balcony of her house onto the rocks one midnight."

"How awful!"

"Yes, miss. Carson Blythe hasn't been good for much since. He lives on there with his adopted daughter, Grace, and his servants, but he's more like a ghost these days than a man."

"You surely know a lot of shocking stories," Norah said, taking a sip of her hot coffee.

"Simple facts. This has been a place of dark shadows for years," the maid told her.

"I'm sure much of it can be put down to superstition," Norah said. "I've helped my father search for sunken treasure for quite a few years now. Sometimes I've actually entered the sunken hulls of wrecks, seen skeletons in their holds, moved around in that strange silent world of deep water and I've never been haunted by a single ghost."

"I'm glad to hear that," Lucy said "Just the same you be careful here."

"I will."

"And don't depend too much on that Barnabas Collins, either," Lucy warned her. "He lives there in that old house and no one ever sees him in the daytime. Willie Loomis won't let a soul into the house."

"He doesn't have any visitors in the days?"

"Never. And it's always dusk or later before Barnabas Collins shows himself. But he wanders around most of the night. Dad saw him standing on the docks one morning when he went down around four o'clock to see about some of the fishing nets that had to be mended. And there was Barnabas standing there in the pitch dark staring out at the ocean."

"He may like the night and solitude."

"So do bats," Lucy said grimly. "But I don't fancy them for company."

Norah didn't like the implied comparison, she decided. She said, "I've finished with the tray. You may as well take it along with you."

"Yes, miss." Lucy covered the tray with a napkin and lifted it from the table. "You'll find Collinwood is a pretty spot in daylight, in spite of everything. The view of the cliffs and bay is grand."

Norah looked mildly amused. "Thanks for leaving me with a pleasant thought. That helps."

"Yes, miss," the stout girl said, and she went on out. At once Norah locked the door and began to prepare for bed. The storm lashed against her windows; according to the weather predictions it would be morning before it subsided.

It occurred to Norah that from the moment she'd entered the old mansion she'd sensed a kind of brooding atmosphere. The elder members of the Collins family had seemed nervous and continually on edge.

Slipping between the sheets, she dismissed these thoughts as nonsense brought on by the girl's superstition. Within a few minutes she had dropped off into a deep slumber.

A banging shutter awakened her; it must have come loose in the storm. She stared up into the darkness and listened to it, wondering if someone would take care of it. If not, she would surely find it hard to sleep again.

She raised herself on an elbow and as she did she thought she saw a movement in the darkness near the foot of her bed. Her heart almost stopped with fear. She gasped and stared at the spot and now was able to make out a figure, tall, motionless, terrifying in its silence. As she watched in horror, the figure suddenly moved toward her. And much as she wanted to scream, she couldn't. She was helpless. . . .

CHAPTER 3

Her terror subsided abruptly; at last she knew who the intruder was. "Barnabas!" she gasped.

The handsome face showed no expression as he hovered over her in the shadows, then bent down, very slowly, and touched his lips to her throat. With a deep sigh she lay back on the pillow as his cold lips continued to press against her skin. A sense of relaxation surged through her and the last of her fear was dispelled. She felt herself sinking into a deep slumber. The black velvet closed in all around her.

When she finally opened her eyes it was daylight and the sun was seeping in around the drapes of her windows. It took her a short time to come fully awake. And then she sat up with a start as she recalled the visit of Barnabas in the night.

Yet it seemed impossible that it had happened. She'd locked the door. There was no way anyone could enter her room. And Barnabas Collins had been so silent and strange! She was sure now it was a dream, a fantastic dream.

Deciding on a red wool pantsuit, she rose and dressed. She'd barely finished when there was a knock on her door. When she opened it she saw Lucy holding a breakfast tray.

"Am I too early, miss?"

"Not at all," Norah said. "But I could easily have gone down to the dining room for my breakfast."

"Mrs. Stoddard takes the morning meal in her room," the maid said. "And she thought you might like it as well."

"It is a luxury," Norah acknowledged with a smile.

As Lucy put the tray down she glanced directly at. Norah and a startled expression crossed her fat face. "Did you sleep well, miss?"

Puzzled by the change in the girl's manner, she said, "Why, yes, for the most part. Why do you ask?"

"I just wondered," the stout girl said, blushing. "I noticed you have a red mark on your throat."

She frowned. "I do?"

"Yes, miss."

Norah turned and went over to check in the oval dresser mirror. Lucy was right. There surely was a small red mark on her neck—an insect bite or even a skin eruption. She touched it with the point of her forefinger and it was slightly itchy.

"You're right, of course," she said, turning to stare at the maid again. "I have no idea what caused the mark."

"You had no bad dreams?" Lucy asked.

It was her turn to blush. She said, "As a matter of fact I did have a minor nightmare. I blame it on the excitement of the evening. I dreamed I saw Mr. Barnabas Collins. I thought he was here in my room. But that had to be impossible."

"Yes, miss." There was a suggestion of doubt in the maid's tone. "Will there be anything else?"

"Thank you, no," Norah said and the girl went out of the bedroom, leaving her alone.

She slowly sank into the chair by the table with a troubled expression on her pretty face. She'd not wanted to go into the details of her dream with the maid. But the after-midnight visit of Barnabas, the mysterious kiss on her throat and the red mark left there all seemed to be linked. A frightening thought crossed her mind. Had there been truth in the Barnabas story? And was the mark on her neck one left by a vampire? She refused to allow herself to think any more about it.

Surely she felt no worse for the nightmare—perhaps a trifle dizzy, but some coffee would cure that. Otherwise she was fine. But when she finished breakfast she went to the dresser and covered the spot with make-up. That would prevent any speculation as to how it came there. When she went downstairs she discovered Carolyn in the living room, reading the Bangor morning paper. Carolyn put the paper aside and rose with a smile to greet her.

"Good morning. Your father has been down to breakfast and he's already left with Uncle Roger to get the car. One of the factory trucks is coming to pull it out of the ditch."

"We are being a lot of nuisance," Norah apologized.

"Not at all," Carolyn said. "I wanted to let you know that the car and your luggage should soon get here."

"It's wonderful news. Thanks," Norah said. "I think I'll go out and take a stroll to view the grounds while I'm waiting."

"You'll find it well worth the effort," the other girl assured her. "I think we have one of the most beautiful locations along the entire Maine coast."

They chatted a moment or two longer before Norah left to move on to the garden. Her mind kept returning to Lucy's startled look and the mark she'd found on her throat. Of course Lucy had upset her with her large store of ghostly gossip. This had put her in a frame of mind to expect phantoms. She stood staring beyond the cliffs at the calm blue water of the cove. Somewhere beneath its surface lay the ancient pirate ship with her holds crammed with looted treasure.

After a while she turned almost automatically toward a path that led past Collinwood and the bams to a distant red brick building. There was never any doubt in her mind that this was the old house to which Barnabas had referred. Nor was there any question concerning her feelings regarding the good-looking cousin of the Collins family. The tall, gaunt Barnabas had made a deeper impression on her mind than any man she'd ever met.

Strolling along the path in the bright spring sunshine, she assured herself that all Lucy's stories of vampires, werewolves and ghosts had been the outpourings of a superstitious and ignorant mind. She'd heard these tales from her father and the other villagers and it excited her to believe them. In the storm and darkness of the previous night Norah too had been credulous, but not oil this pleasant morning.

The grass was still dull and withered from the cold of winter and the trees had not yet begun to come into leaf, so the landscape was touched with drabness. Yet the evergreens remained and the blue hills and ocean to contrast with the gray of the cliffs. It was an interesting country now and, she decided, must be truly delightful in summer.

She paused at the entrance to the old house. It's dark shutters were closed as if it weren't occupied and there was no sign of life about the place. She moved on by the house to note the field beyond and a distant cemetery at the bottom of it. Then she gave her attention to the dark vehicle parked by the house. This was the station wagon which belonged to Barnabas.

Studying it, she was convinced it had once been a hearse, but now its interior had been converted to that of a station wagon. She peered in its windows, but saw no sign of the coffin which she'd thought she'd seen there the night before. No doubt she'd been wrong in that.

She was still staring inside the wagon when a voice behind her asked, "What are you doing here?"

Turning, she was confronted by the loutish features of the youth whom Barnabas had called Willie Loomis. The young man was studying her with some hostility.

She managed a smile. "I came here to see Mr. Collins."

"He ain't seeing anyone," Willie Loomis said.

"Will you tell him Norah Bliss is here?" she asked. "I have an idea he'll make an exception in my case."

He shook his head. "I have my orders," he said stubbornly. "You're wasting your time."

She stared at him. "You won't even take my message to him?"

"Mr. Barnabas doesn't wish to be disturbed in the daytime," the young man said. "He is at work."

"What sort of work?"

"Mr. Barnabas is writing a history of Collinwood," Loomis said. "Everyone knows that."

"I didn't," she told him. "You must remember I'm a stranger here."

"You'll find out Mr. Barnabas has his own ways. If you want to talk to him, he'll be available after dinner tonight."

"I see," she said. "Thank you for the information."

Willie Loomis looked stern. "You keep bothering us here and you'll only bring trouble on yourself."

She felt her face crimson, but she said coolly, "I have no intention of making a nuisance of myself. Now that I understand, I'll not try to contact Barnabas until he's free of his work. You can at least tell him I've called when you're talking with him."

"I'll tell him later, miss." And with that he walked away and up the entrance steps to enter the oaken door of the old house! It closed after him with a slam.

Surprised and embarrassed, Norah returned to the grounds of Collinwood. Since her father had not yet come with the car, she decided to take the path down the cliffs to the small wharf. The path was steep enough to make her go slowly. When she reached the rocky beach she strolled across to the wharf. It was about twenty-five feet square and of weathered timbers. This would be where much of their activity would center.

A light cabin cruiser was tied at the end of the wharf; probably this belonged to Roger Collins, she guessed.

She turned to stare up at the cliffs and found they rose so steeply that they cut off any view of Collinwood. Shifting her gaze down along the beach, she saw a distant house built out on the rock face that answered Lucy's description of the contemporary mansion belonging to Carson Blythe. At the same time she saw two figures, a man and a woman, slowly strolling along the narrow beach toward the wharf where she was standing.

As they drew close to the wharf she saw that the man was a thin, frail type with horn-rimmed glasses, white hair, and fine, ascetic features. He wore a gray sports coat and dark flannel trousers. The girl at his side was young enough to be his daughter. She had a round, pretty face, sparkling blue eyes, and titian hair. She had on a modish suede coat with white slacks showing beneath it.

The man came out on the wharf and with a bleak smile said, "You are also enjoying the beach on this pleasant morning?"

"Yes," she said, returning his smile. "This is my first day at Collinwood and I'm trying to get a complete impression of the place."

He looked at her with new interest. "Then you must be Miss Bliss, the daughter of Claude Bliss, who is due here to try and salvage the treasure from *The Jenny Swift*?"

"I am," she said, surprised that he should know all about her. Apparently the word had gotten around.

He must have noted her surprise for he quickly explained, "I'm Carson Blythe. I own the house you see a little way down the cliffs. I'm especially interested in your venture since I attempted to wrest the treasure from that old pirate ship myself."

"Of course," she said. "I've read about you."

"No doubt," he said rather bleakly. The red-haired young woman had come up beside him and he introduced her, saying, "This is my adopted daughter, Grace, Miss Norah Bliss."

Grace offered her a slim, tanned hand. "Welcome, Miss Bliss. I hope you have luck with the treasure."

"More than I did, at any rate," was Carson Blythe's bitter comment. "You say you've read about my exploration. So you must know about the curse and what it did to me?"

She felt embarrassed. "I'm not too familiar with the details."

Carson Blythe said, "I think you should be, so you'll know what you're getting into."

Grace Blythe touched her father's arm in an apparent attempt to restrain him. "There's no need to go into all that at this time, father!" she pleaded.

The white-haired man glared at her from behind his thick horn-rimmed glasses. "Now I must disagree," he said. "I only wish I had someone to warn me. Your mother might still be alive!"

Grace Blythe's face shadowed. It was clear she had little control over her foster father. "You'll only upset yourself going over it all."

Norah felt embarrassed. Not knowing what to do or say, she stared at the waves lapping hungrily against the wharf. The air turned cool as the sun temporarily slipped behind a cloud.

Carson Blythe's thin face showed pain. "I'm sure the curse upon that wreck out there is real. I've seen the horror of Jenny Swift's ghost myself. And I know what it can do. She came to taunt me and my late wife until one moonlight night my wife hurled herself from our balcony onto the rocks."

"I'm sorry," Norah murmured.

Carson Blythe frowned. "The day I decided to try and take the fortune from *The Jenny Swift* I sealed my wife's fate. Grace can tell you!"

"It's not anything we should discuss with Miss Bliss."

"I say it is," Carson Blythe went on, his voice showing deep emotion. "You can see I'm a haunted man, Miss Bliss. I lost a fortune in equipment when the storm came at the height of our search for the treasure. And do you know what we recovered for all the expense and effort? Three rusty trunks containing iron locks and lengths of chain! From the start of our salvage efforts the ghost of Jenny Swift tormented us! I've seen her face with its horrible, mutilated right cheek! I know what her malicious, avenging spirit can do!"

"Thank you for the warning," Norah said quietly at the end of the tirade. "I doubt if it will make any difference to my father. He doesn't believe in ghosts. Nor, I'm afraid, do I."

"You see?" Grace said, plainly upset. "I said you would be wasting your time."

Carson Blythe shrugged. "At least my conscience is clear. I have told you the truth as I've known it, Miss Bliss."

"I understand that," she said. "And I appreciate it."

"My great loss has made me touchy on the subject," he admitted. "But let me warn you my late wife was as self-assured and normal as yourself before that evil thing came to torment us."

"I'll tell my father that we've met," Norah said. "I'm sure he'd enjoy meeting you and hearing the details of your salvage attempt."

The old man looked bitter. "I'm afraid it would make for grim listening. Still, I do want to know your father. You and he are welcome to visit us at any time. Grace and I live quiet lives these days."

Grace smiled at her timidly. "Please do accept the invitation," she said. "We'd enjoy having you."

"Thank you," Norah said. She found the attractive girl likable, yet strangely pathetic—no doubt because of the tragic experiences she'd undergone. Whether her foster mother's death had been attributable to the ghost of Jenny Swift or not, her suicide must have left a scar on all the household.

"When do you plan to begin work?" Blythe asked her.

"Within a few days," she said. "The bathysphere my father designed is going to be towed here from Portsmouth almost at once."

The white-haired man looked interested. "What sort of diving chamber is it?" he asked. "Does it have any special features?"

"It is very easy to manipulate," she said. "And divers can work from it all day and night if necessary. There's air and space enough for two men to remain in it longer than that."

"I had no such luxury equipment," Carson Blythe said with a frown. "It could be your father will have success. But what I ask is whether it is worth it? The ghost of that female pirate will carry out the curse, wait and see!"

Grace said, "My father feels very strongly about this. But you mustn't be discouraged."

"I understand," Norah said.

"We'll see you at your convenience then, Miss Bliss," Carson Blythe said sternly. "Give my best wishes to your father." And with that he turned and strode off the wharf with the titian-haired girl at his side. They went down along the beach without looking back.

Norah waited until they were a distance away before leaving the wharf and making her way up the path again. At least she was meeting some of the neighbors. It had been interesting to talk to Carson Blythe, though she considered him a tragic, broken-hearted person. Grace also had a strange appeal. She would have to arrange with her father to visit them, for Carson Blythe's information concerning his search for the sunken treasure would come in useful.

When she reached the lawns before Collinwood she saw that their car was parked out in front of the great mansion. Her father had driven it back. The housekeeper informed her that all her luggage had been taken up to her room. So Norah at once went upstairs to unpack. She was still busy at this when her father came to spend a few minutes with her.

"The car had no damage beyond being well caked with mud," he told her.

"I'm glad," she said. "It might not be easy to get it repaired here."

"I understand there is a good garage at Ellsworth. How do you think you're going to like staying here?"

"I think it's very pleasant." They were standing by the window of the room overlooking the ocean. "I have a lovely view from here."

Her father nodded. "I'll be glad when the equipment and crew arrive and we can get started."

"I know," she said. "I met Carson Blythe down on the wharf with his adopted daughter." And she went on to give him the details of the meeting and the conversation which followed.

Her father's intelligent face took on a frown. "He must have very strong opinions about the curse and Jenny Swift's ghost," he said, when she had finished.

"He has," she agreed. "I'm afraid his daughter was embarrassed."

"Of course he had very bad luck between the storm and his wife's suicide," her father said. "And you say he claims to have recovered nothing of value in the ancient trunks he salvaged."

"That is what he said."

"It's possible," her father agreed. "He could have found a working area of the old vessel rather than the hold where the treasure caskets were kept. By all accounts *the Jenny Swift* was loaded with gold bullion and precious jewels taken from ships on the Spanish Main."

She gave him a worried look. "Could it all be merely legend?"

"I think not," Claude Bliss said. "There are strong indications that what I've told you is true. Evidently Roger Collins and his friends have enough faith in the venture to want to offer financial backing and share in the possible gains."

Her eyes met his solemnly. "What about the curse?"

"The legend that anyone who tries to recover the treasure shall suffer?" He smiled. "You know how many such wrecks we've worked on and almost every one of them had some such legend attached to it."

"But in Carson Blythe's case, at least, the curse seems to have been real enough."

"That is the way he sees it. He likely would have had the same bad luck anyway."

"He claims he's seen Jenny Swift's ghost."

"In his frame of mind, any shadow could be the ghost."

"Perhaps," she said. "Just the same, I'm worried."

"You'll hear a lot of superstitious talk and legends in a coastal village like this," her father pointed out. "You've already had a sample of this in what was said about Barnabas last night. I feel the comments about him were most unfair."

"I agree."

"But the gossip will continue," her father said. "We can only protect ourselves by ignoring it. I have come here to salvage that sunken treasure and nothing is going to stand in my way."

So that was that. When she mentioned Carson Blythe's invitation, he agreed it would be interesting to visit the eccentric millionaire and learn more details of the ill-fated salvage operation he'd attempted.

The balance of the day passed quickly. When Norah went downstairs for dinner she paused in the entrance foyer to study the portrait of the first Barnabas Collins. What Carolyn had told her was true; the present Barnabas was almost his double.

"That's the one who turned into a vampire bat." It was young David who had joined her and volunteered this bit of information.

She turned to the youngster and smiled. "Do you mean that literally?"

"Sure," David said. "He could change shape whenever he liked. One minute he'd be walking around the grounds and the next he'd be a bat flying out over the ocean."

"Where did you hear such a story?"

"Everyone knows that," David boasted. "Ask Lucy or any of the servants. They'll tell you his ghost still comes around here as a bat occasionally."

"I find that hard to believe," she protested.

David looked at her oddly. "Are you sweet on Barnabas?" he demanded, with boyish directness.

She blushed. "I hardly know him. But he seems nice."

"He's all right," the boy said. "But they tell some pretty tall stories about him. He likes to wander in graveyards at night. And some say he's a vampire like the Barnabas in that painting."

"I don't think such talk is worthy of being listened to," she said with some disdain.

"Maybe not," David said frankly. "But I tell you I don't ever go out by myself at night."

Norah was glad when they were summoned into the dining room to join the others. Roger Collins presided at the dinner table and it proved a pleasant, uneventful meal. Afterward they went to the living room to await the arrival of Dr. Julia Hoffman and Professor Stokes, the others interested in forming a company to back the salvage attempt.

Meanwhile dusk had arrived and night was settling in. Norah hadn't long to wonder about whether Barnabas would put in an appearance; soon the doorbell rang and the handsome man in the caped coat was ushered into the living room. He was greeted with a modest welcome and almost at once went over to join her.

"How do you like Collinwood after a day to get used to it?" he wanted to know.

"I find it interesting," she said, looking up into his gaunt face. "I tried to reach you this morning but your servant wouldn't deliver my message to you."

Barnabas sighed. "I'm sorry about that, but you mustn't blame poor Willie. He is only doing what I instructed. I'm engaged in an important project during the daylight hours and don't like to be disturbed."

"So I hear," she said. "You're something of a historian."

"I have ambitions in that direction," Barnabas said. "So I ask you to be tolerant of me."

She smiled. "I'll try to be."

At that point Dr. Julia Hoffman and Professor Stokes arrived. The female doctor was an interesting type, possessed of charm and a certain kind of worn good looks. Her associate, Professor Stokes, was a bluff, portly Englishman. Norah and her father were introduced to them both. And when Dr. Hoffman went over to talk privately to Barnabas, Norah was aware of the deep interest the woman had in him. Indeed, it struck Norah that Julia Hoffman was probably in love with the handsome Collins cousin.

Professor Stokes took the floor in the center of the room to begin the discussion. "I'm sure we're all happy to have Mr. Bliss and his lovely daughter with us—not only because their company is welcome, but also because they offer us our best opportunity to end the legend of *the Jenny Swift* and recover the treasure from that ancient vessel."

"Hear, hear!" Roger said solemnly.

The professor looked pleased. "Thank you, Roger. We surely agree that too much loose talk has been circulated about the sunken vessel, the treasure and the curse that surrounds it. With the aid of Claude Bliss and his new bathysphere I am convinced the curse will be broken and the treasure brought up from the ocean depths."

Norah's father smiled. "We'll at least make a good try."

"I'm sure of that," Professor Stokes said, his florid face beaming. "We are ready to back you with hard dollars. And I have confidence it will be an investment well repaid."

Elizabeth Stoddard spoke from her chair by the fireplace. "At least let us settle the mystery surrounding the wreck."

Julia nodded agreement. "A great deal of interest has been aroused by this new venture to solve that mystery."

Professor Stokes sighed. "Carson Blythe's tragic experience caused a lot of panicky talk—talk which I feel should be ignored. We are all familiar with the story of how the ship was heading into this cove one stormy night nearly three centuries ago in search of shelter. Commanded by one of the few women pirates ever to sail under the skull and crossbones, it wasn't a happy ship. Jenny Swift was as cruelly arrogant as she was beautiful, if the historical accounts are correct. The crew wanted to abandon the vessel but she forbade it."

Carolyn's face was bright with excitement. "I've always pictured her as brave and lovely, holding sway over her crew of cutthroats with that fabulous blacksnake whip she supposedly used as a weapon."

Professor Stokes looked mildly amused. "That is the romantic story we have heard about her," he agreed. "But I think the truth is that she was a cruel, heartless amazon. She did flourish the long blacksnake whip even to the end when the ship sank with all on board that stormy long-ago February night. And in the last moments of the wreck, her face was crushed by a falling mast. It is that crushed, horrible face the ghost fanciers describe."

From a shadowed corner of the big room to which he'd retreated, Barnabas spoke up. "Are you suggesting, Professor Stokes, that those who claim to have seen the ghost are lying?"

"I doubt if such a ghost has ever existed," Professor Stokes said. "I put it down to imagination and the nervous fears of the superstitious."

"Indeed," Barnabas said, in a solemn voice. "Then isn't it odd that the first man ever to attempt to recover the treasure was found washed up on the Collinwood beach with what appeared to be the welt of a whip around his neck?"

CHAPTER 4

There was a hush in the big, softly-lighted room for a moment. Then Professor Stokes awkwardly cleared his throat and said, "I'm familiar with that story, but I have never quite believed it."

"Strange," Barnabas said. "I had it on good authority."

Roger Collins, who was standing in front of the fireplace, gave Barnabas a defiant look. "I know the legend has come down through the years, that every victim of the curse dies with a welt around his or her neck. I even heard the claim made in the case of Carson Blythe's wife. When they discovered her body after she'd killed herself it was whispered widely that her throat showed a strange mark all the way around it."

"And wasn't it true?" Barnabas asked in his quiet manner.

"I really don't know," Roger said irritably. "From what I was told of the state of the body when it was found, no one could be sure."

"Exactly," Professor Stokes said. "I say forget all the ghost talk and remain with the facts, the most important of which is that Mr. Bliss has perfected a new diving bell which will make it much easier to work around the wreck. With its use I see no reason why we shouldn't meet with success."

"It surely sounds hopeful," Elizabeth Stoddard observed with a smile and she turned to Norah's father. "Are you equally optimistic,

Mr. Bliss?"

"Yes. I'd say so. I have never paid any attention to the many ghost stories. We hear them every time we approach a sunken vessel. I don't feel we should have any problems in the present instance, once we get the diving bell lowered to the exact location of *the Jenny Swift*. From then on it should be relatively simple."

This brought a lot of questions from the others concerning the operations. Both Norah and her father tried to explain the benefits of the new bathysphere. And finally the discussion came to an end with Elizabeth having coffee and cakes served for everyone.

Norah moved over to the shadowed corner where Barnabas had taken his stand. Looking up into his gaunt face, she said, "I was interested in your comments."

He seemed grimly amused. "I'm afraid I wasn't popular with the professor or the others."

"Do you actually believe in the ghost of this beautiful female pirate who carries a long blacksnake whip?"

Barnabas looked at her with his deep-set eyes. "Haven't you been here long enough to sense there is something different about this place? Yes, I do believe Collinwood has its phantoms."

"Including that of Jenny Swift?"

"I've never been sure. That's why the question fascinates me."

"Don't you approve of our treasure hunt?"

"I thought I made myself clear on that score last night," Barnabas said. "I wish you all good luck. But I worry when pompous idiots like the professor try to minimize the hazards of such a venture."

"My father and I are all too aware of them," she said. "And we're also familiar with the type of easy optimism the professor represents. We've managed before and we will this time."

"I hope so," Barnabas said. "It worries me that Carson Blythe met such disaster in his efforts. I would feel bad if a similar fate should overtake your expedition."

"Then you do think the curse is real?"

"Let me put it this way," Barnabas said. "I have seen a number of people meet dire fates when they tried to challenge it."

"I suppose it could happen again," Norah admitted ruefully. "Call it a hazard of our profession."

At this point Professor Stokes came beaming up with his coffee cup in hand. He began with, "Your father tells me you spent some months in Greek waters last year. What an experience that must have been. The ancient vessels you must have come upon in those ocean depths. I know the area well and have been skin-diving there."

"How interesting," she said, politely, though she'd much

preferred to have continued her quiet talk with Barnabas.

But the gregarious professor was not to be easily discouraged. "Tell me something about your experiences," he begged.

She strained to think of something, then said, "When we were working on the salvage of an ancient wreck off Porquerolles we came upon an octopus city on a flat shallow ocean floor. We could hardly believe what we saw. But the octopus lives in crannies of rock and reed. And this was a gathering place for them."

Professor Stokes turned the conversation to the wreck of *the Jenny Swift*. "There are some strong currents in the area," he advised. "You will have to take them into account."

"Father has an excellent crew used to such problems," she promised.

Dr. Julia Hoffman came to them with a smile on her attractive face. "I see you two are not finding any difficulty in communicating."

"On the contrary," Professor Stokes said. "This young lady has a fascinating lore of information about life under the sea."

"You must tell me about some of your adventures," Dr. Hoffman said.

"They are not all that fascinating," she protested. The professor had moved on to talk to Roger and so she and Julia Hoffman were by themselves. She asked, "How far away is your hospital?"

"About a forty-minute drive," Julia said. "I don't mind the distance. I come here quite often." She glanced across the room at Barnabas, who was chatting with Norah's father. "At one time Barnabas was my patient."

"Oh?" Norah said.

The doctor sighed. "He resented the time he had to sacrifice for medical attention and so gave up coming to the hospital. I have always felt bad about it."

"Is his health still not what it should be?" Norah asked with some concern.

Julia became wary. "He is not a well person. His condition isn't critical, but it is chronic."

"Can't you persuade him to take up treatments under you again?"

"I wish I could. But I've given up."

Norah's gaze shifted to Barnabas once again. "He is such a nice person."

A look that could have been one of jealousy crossed Julia's face. "I was watching you two when I first arrived. I could tell that you're very taken with him."

"I think he's a fine man."

"Don't allow yourself to become too interested in him," the

doctor warned her. "It could lead to heartbreak for you. Barnabas leads a lonely and very special life. Romance is never likely to become part of it."

She blushed at the older woman's bluntness; again she had the feeling that Julia Hoffman was in love with Barnabas and jealous of a younger woman showing him attention. She was saved from having to continue the conversation when Roger Collins came up to join them.

She greeted him warmly, and said, "I was about to ask Dr. Hoffman to tell me more about her hospital."

"Yes," Roger said with a friendly glance at the woman doctor. "Julia has engaged in some remarkable research at her place. And she has been responsible for some miraculous cures."

"Not precisely miraculous, but thank you," Julia said smoothly. "I do wish that Barnabas hadn't ceased to come to me for his treatments."

Roger's face shadowed. "I believe Barnabas doesn't want to regain his health. He appears to be quite content to remain as he is."

"Which is wrong," the doctor said.

"Assuredly," Roger Collins agreed sternly.

Norah wanted very much to ask what Barnabas' mysterious malady was but she knew the question would be untactful.

Eventually Dr. Hoffman and Professor Stokes announced their departure. And Norah didn't miss that Julia Hoffman went over to Barnabas and talked to him in an earnest fashion before she left. Barnabas appeared to be trying to humor her but he showed no great interest in whatever she was saying. Then with a final smile for him she moved on. A few minutes later, she and the Professor left.

Elizabeth and Carolyn went up to bed, while Norah's father and Roger Collins retreated to Roger's study down the hall. This left Norah alone in the living room with Barnabas.

"I must go now as well," he said.

She gave him a teasing look. "Surely you can't have appointments at this hour of the night?"

He smiled. "No. But it is late. Folk here at Collinwood retire early."

"I'm used to different hours," she confessed.

"So am I," he said. "But the local people don't understand that."

"Dr. Hoffman is very much interested in you."

"You think so?"

"Without a question," she said. "I can tell by the way she looks at you and the things she says about you. She mentioned you were a patient of hers once. She worries that you gave up too soon."

Barnabas looked annoyed. "The woman has no right to

discuss that with anyone. I gave up my treatments because I felt she wasn't helping me."

"A logical reason," Norah said with a small smile. "Have you tried any other doctors?"

"I've been to a number of specialists," Barnabas said. "But really it's nothing to be concerned about I don't consider it worth discussing."

Her eyes met his. "You should be careful of your health."

He nodded. "And you should be careful of this place," he warned her. "You may be letting yourself in for more than you realize."

"You sound very forbidding."

"Sorry. But I've promised you I'd be frank."

"I hope you won't think me silly," she said, "but last night I had a strange nightmare and you were in it"

He stared at her. "I was in it?"

"Yes. I looked up and you were standing by my bed. Then you bent down and touched your lips to my throat. After that I sank into some kind of a deep sleep and didn't awake until this morning."

"Have you told this to anyone?" he asked.

"Yes. When I woke up I mentioned it to the maid. And she pointed out I had a mark on my throat. And so I had. It must have been some sort of insect sting bothering me which triggered off the nightmare."

Barnabas looked relieved. "A reasonable explanation."

"I warned you it was an odd dream," she laughed. "But I wanted to tell you about it."

His eyes fixed on her gently. "I'm glad to be included in your dreams," he said. "But I don't think I'd repeat the story. Others might not understand."

"I don't intend to tell anyone else."

"Wise girl," he said. "I'll see you tomorrow night or some other night soon. And in the meanwhile, you'll be advancing with your plans for the salvage."

"Yes," she said as she went to the door with him. "I met Carson Blythe today and found him very strange. I suppose the tragedy has crushed him."

"He's not a happy man."

"Grace seems nice, though. And she's pretty."

"The Blythes were not the proper sort to adopt her," Barnabas said. "It would have been better if it hadn't happened."

"The suicide must have changed their lives."

"Undoubtedly," Barnabas said. "And now I really must go."

With a solemn smile he bent and touched his lips to her forehead. His lips felt strangely cold. Then he said, "Remember, you may be in great danger before your mission here is accomplished."

"I'll remember," she promised. She remained at the open door as he walked off into the darkness. When he'd gone a short distance he turned and waved. Then he vanished in the shadows.

With a sigh she closed the door. He was the most unusual man she'd ever met. Just being with him gave her a certain warm feeling and yet there was something dreadfully sad about him. When the opportunity presented itself she must question Carolyn Stoddard about this charming British cousin. She was sure there was more to his story than she yet knew.

She went straight upstairs and prepared for bed. Sleep came readily enough. But with it there also came the same dream of the previous night, which troubled her vaguely when she awakened the following morning. Before Lucy came with her breakfast tray she went to the mirror to check her throat. The red mark was there, as vivid as ever. Quickly she found the proper make-up to cover the spot so the girl would ask no awkward questions.

It was a dull day with the threat of rain. Her father received a phone call from Portsmouth informing him the tug was on its way with the bathysphere and the special scow. She was seated in the study with him going over their plan of operation when Carolyn came to them with a puzzled look on her face. She said, "There's a couple waiting in the living room to talk with you two."

Norah's father asked, "Are they local people?"

"No," Carolyn said. "They said that their name is Cartill, and that they've just rented the cottage on the estate road for the summer."

Claude Bliss was standing. "And they want to talk to me?"

"Yes," Carolyn said. "They asked about you and Norah."

She smiled and turned to her father. "I suppose we should see them. They may be newspaper people here to follow our salvage of *The Jenny Swift*."

Carolyn's face brightened. "Of course. I should have guessed. They're both quite young."

Norah's father said, "We'll go talk with them."

She and her father went directly to the living room where a tiny dark girl with a swarthy type of beauty sat demurely. By her side a smartly dressed young man stood.

He had wavy brown hair, sideburns and a goatee. Seeing them, he came over with his hand outstretched.

"Mr. Claude Bliss and Miss Norah," he said with a charming smile. "I'm happy to meet you. I am David Cartill and this is my wife, Belle." He turned to the dark woman and she smiled faintly but did not rise.

Norah's father said, "I understand you have rented a cottage on the estate for the summer."

"Yes," David Cartill replied. "Mr. Roger Collins was kind enough to rent it to us."

"What is your business here and why does it concern us?" Claude Bliss wanted to know.

Cartill smiled. "My wife and I have lived in the West Indies most of our lives—Barbados, to be exact. If you will recall, that is where the pirate Jenny Swift had her island headquarters."

"Rumor says so," her father agreed.

"I'm sure it was true," Cartill assured him. He glanced at the quiet dark girl again. "As a matter of fact, that is why my wife and I are here."

"Indeed?" Bliss said. "My daughter guessed you might have some interest in our salvage operation."

"I surely have," Cartill assured them, his eyes dancing with some hidden inner delight.

"Are you from the newspapers?" Norah ventured.

"No," the young man said urbanely, his hands behind him. "At home on the island my profession is the law."

"You are a lawyer," her father said.

"I am." David Cartill smiled, seeming to be thoroughly enjoying himself. "And that brings me to our business." He paused.

"Please go on," Norah's father said with some impatience.

"It's about your proposal to raise the treasure from the sunken vessel Jenny Swift. I'm afraid I may have to interfere with your salvage operation unless we can come to terms."

Claude Bliss looked shocked. "What are you talking about?"

The young man kept his good humor. "Very simple, sir," he said with a wide gesture. "My good wife here is a direct descendant of Jenny Swift. Jenny had a legitimate son who spent his life in Barbados. We can prove the line of descent. So my wife, you see, is the legitimate heir to any treasure found on the vessel owned by her ancestor."

Norah was thunderstruck and she could see that her father was just as surprised. "Why didn't you come forward with your claim before?"

He lifted his eyebrows. "Only when you people announced you were coming to Collinwood to search for the wreck did we learn about *The Jenny Swift*. Naturally, we lost no time flying up here to be on the scene and protect our interests."

Norah's father swallowed hard. "Am I to understand that you're going to take some legal action to interfere with our starting the operation?"

Cartill continued in his friendly fashion, "I wouldn't like to prevent your getting underway. After all, if you do find anything it is to the advantage of all of us. But I must stress that we shall have to come to terms."

Norah stared at him. "You're saying we'll have to share our findings with your wife and you."

"Yes," he said. "The moment you come up with a worthwhile find I'll go into the courts and restrain you from doing anything with it until my wife's claim is settled. Naturally, I would prefer that we work out our differences without turning to the law. But that is your decision."

Claude Bliss' thin, intelligent face showed anger and dismay. "Before I talk to you at all, I'll have my own lawyers check your background in Barbados and be sure who we're dealing with."

"That is only reasonable," David Cartill said amiably.

"This will take time," Norah's father warned him. "And I'll not expect you to cause any trouble during the period we're investigating your claim."

"We shall stand by as interested observers ... at least until the moment you bring up some treasure. Then I'll proceed as outlined."

"I don't like your threats," her father told him angrily.

Cartill looked wounded. "I'm surprised at your attitude, sir," he said with great sincerity. "My wife and I feel we are being most fair in this matter."

Norah said bitterly, "You're offering a threat to our entire project."

The young man smiled again. "You forget it is we who are the wronged parties. It is my wife who should inherit all the fortune once owned by her infamous ancestor."

"Then let her collect it at the bottom of the ocean," Norah's father said bitterly.

"That is of course, the crux of the matter. You are equipped to rescue the treasure. And we are willing to share it with you. Most generous on our part. Don't you agree?"

Bliss glared at him. "How do I know that you and your wife aren't confidence crooks, here to bluff us into sharing any treasure we find with you?"

"Cruel of you to show so little regard for my dear Belle's feelings," the young man murmured. "But I can understand you are a trifle upset. We shall be at the cottage whenever you wish to contact us. We intend to keep a close eye on the salvage operation." He turned to his wife. "Come, Belle, I see no point in our remaining here any longer."

The dark girl got up and they both went to the front door and out. When Norah's father closed the door after them, he turned to her and asked, "What do you make of that?"

She was angry. "It's a swindle. Why would Roger Collins rent the cottage to them?"

"I can't imagine," her father said with a troubled sigh, "unless he didn't know what they were up to."

And this turned out to be exactly the situation. When the head of the Collins clan returned that evening and heard their story he went into a rage. "That young scoundrel!" he exclaimed. "He didn't let on what he was doing here. He said they wanted to rest here for the summer months. I'll find some way to break the lease and get rid of him."

"No," Norah's father said. "I wouldn't do that. There's a tiny chance he may have some legal claim to the treasure. Until I make a thorough check through my lawyer, we'd better let him remain where he is."

"They won't bother you?" Roger asked.

"No more than they already have," Norah's father said. "I'm so certain this is a confidence trick I'm not too concerned."

"I still don't like having them on the estate," Roger said. "But I'll do as you suggest."

"Thank you," Claude Bliss said, his thin face thoughtful. "It's strange."

"What?" Roger asked.

"I'm almost ready to believe the famed curse is at work. This is a most unpleasant development."

Roger looked grim. "Regarding the curse," he said, "I had a visit from Carson Blythe today at my office. He came to talk to me about the treasure hunt. Up until now I had no idea what a bad mental state he's in. He begged me not to allow you to go ahead with the salvage."

"Why?" her father asked.

"We're back to the curse," Roger said with some exasperation. "It seems Blythe believes we'll all suffer from some calamity if we press on with the search for treasure."

"He said that to me," Norah recalled.

"The man is obviously insane on the subject," Roger complained. "And I as much as told him so and sent him on his way."

"You did the right thing," her father said.

Dusk finally came and she began to feel restless. After the unsettling day she wanted to talk to Barnabas and ask his advice. After dinner, the family had gathered in the living room as usual, and as soon as the chance arose, she slipped out of the room, grabbed her coat and let herself out into the dark night.

It was cool, without any hint of stars. In the distance she could hear the pounding of the waves. It was lonely and she knew she was going against the very warning which Barnabas had given her. But he'd not promised to come to Collinwood, so if she wanted to talk to him her best bet was to go to the old house.

She knew the way from having covered the ground in daylight. As she started across the lawn, she glanced at the living room window and saw her father standing there talking with Elizabeth Stoddard; the others were further in the background. For an instant she had a frightened desire to turn and hurry back into the old mansion, but then she found her courage again.

Rounding the mansion, she started along the path. She could only see a short distance through the shadows and she promised herself if she ever tried this again she'd provide herself with a flashlight at the very least. To the right she could see the beams and some lights in the cottages of the help. Collinwood had grown to be a large estate with quite a few servants working both inside and out

She walked swiftly on, still not able to see any sign of the old house. She wondered what Barnabas would think about the Cartills and their claim. As she thought about this she was suddenly aware of a figure blocking the path ahead of her.

Fear raced through her with chilling speed. She halted, not knowing whether to go on or to turn and run as swiftly as she could back to the mansion. A quick calculation told her she'd not get far in safety. Whoever it was would be almost certain to overtake her. She had no choice but to face the unknown stranger.

She called, "Who is it?"

"No one of importance," came the mocking reply in a voice that she recognized.

"You're David Cartill," she cried out in exasperation.

"Right the first time," he said, coming up to her. "Your perception is remarkable."

"And so is your nerve!" she cried with anger. "You have no right to be wandering here! You're trespassing!"

"Don't phrase it so crudely," he begged her. "Actually being out here is not my idea. I'm searching for my wife. Have you by any chance seen her?"

"No!" She was sure he was lying, that he'd been wandering around to spy on them all.

"Too bad," he said worriedly. "She vanished earlier this evening. She does this sort of thing every so often. Confidentially, she has a fancy for voodoo. Being brought up in the islands she knows all about that sort of thing. And this afternoon she said something about wanting to search out certain herbs to make some potion."

"You're indulging in a witless joke."

"No, honestly," David Cartill said. "These voodoo cultists don't expect to find the herbs they use in daylight. To get them right they have to be discovered under a full moon or in the black of the night."

"I'm not interested," she said uneasily.

"So I'll just keep on searching for her," the young man said. "And what are you doing out here alone?" There was a certain insinuation in his tone that frightened her.

"I'm meeting someone."

He smiled. "I don't see anyone."

"They'll be here in a moment," she lied, praying someone would come along.

"Maybe I ought to protect you in the meanwhile."

"No thank you."

"You sound very definite on that point," he taunted her.

"I am," she said, a terrified tremor in her voice.

He reached out toward her. "After all, I want us to be friends. That's not asking much!"

"Let me be!" she cried, backing away from him.

What David Cartill would have done next she was never to discover. For at that same instant the tall, caped figure of Barnabas emerged from the shadows. He asked sternly, "What's going on here?"

David Cartill gave him a frightened glance over his shoulder. "Not a thing!" And he at once ran off into the darkness in the direction of Collinwood.

Barnabas watched after him with a scowl and then came to her filled with concern. "Are you safe?"

"Yes," she said weakly.

"You know how foolish you are to be out here alone?"

"I do now," she admitted. "That was David Cartill. I was on my way to tell you about him."

Barnabas showed a strange expression on his handsome face. "Is that what he's calling himself this time?"

"What do you mean?"

His deep-set eyes met hers. "I mean his name isn't David Cartill. That was Quentin Collins."

CHAPTER 5

They stood there in the eerie darkness facing each other. She stared at him and echoed, "Quentin Collins?"

"The name means nothing to you?"

"No."

He sighed. "Well, I don't want to keep you standing here while you listen to a long story. And there'll be no chance for us to talk privately if we go to Collinwood."

"No. They're all in the living room," she said. "That is why I decided to slip out by myself and try to find you."

He studied her with worried eyes. "I can understand why you did it," he admitted, "but you should have been more concerned with your own safety. What you had to tell me could have waited."

"I didn't think so."

Barnabas looked back. "There's just one solution. You return to the old house with me. I'll find you a glass of wine. We'll have a talk and then I'll see you safely back to the main house."

She said, "I'm trembling."

"I don't wonder," Barnabas said, placing an arm around her as they started walking on towards the old red building. "Something told me you were out here and in danger."

"I almost collapsed when I saw him blocking my way."

"You should have screamed. If I hadn't heard you, Willie or

someone over at the barns might have."

"I guess I wasn't thinking very logically," she admitted. "When did you first see him?"

"This afternoon. He came to Collinwood with his wife."

"He has no wife," Barnabas said flatly.

"He said she was his wife."

"One of the first things you must learn about my cousin Quentin is not to pay too much attention to what he tells you."

They walked on to the old house and Barnabas opened the front door and showed her in. She had never been inside it before and when she stepped into the living room with its comfortable fire in the fireplace she was much impressed.

Turning to Barnabas, she said, "It's very pleasant, though not as large as the new Collinwood."

He looked pleased. "It has always been my favorite of the two, even though it is not as imposing outside as the new house."

She moved around the room looking at the fine antique furniture and the oil portraits of family ancestors on the wall. Candelabra burned on the mantle and on the table in the center of the room to give it soft but ample light. "You don't have electricity?" she asked.

"No," he said. "I'm here so little. And somehow electric lighting seems out of keeping with this fine old place."

She smiled. "Women generally prefer candlelight. It is so much more flattering."

Barnabas was staring at her with admiring eyes. "You look lovely wherever I see you. Will you have a glass of sherry?"

"That would be very nice," she said, seating herself by the fireplace. "My nerves are still a little upset by that experience I had outside."

"Unfortunate," Barnabas murmured as he filled the sherry glasses from a decanter. Then he brought a glass to her and stood before the fireplace where he could talk and study her.

She sipped the sherry. "It's excellent."

Barnabas held up his own glass to inspect its color. "We have some fine vintage wines in the cellar here. Some of them were overlooked when the family moved to the other house. So I have been reaping the benefits."

"Now tell me more about this Quentin Collins."

The handsome face showed a rueful smile. "Perhaps I should begin by saying that Quentin and myself are the two renegades of the Collins family. We have been the wanderers and the rebels, a disgrace to our more conservative and respectable relatives."

"I'm sure you're most respectable!"

"Don't believe it. As time goes on you're bound to hear more talk about me. I promise you a lot of it won't be favorable. But I doubt if I'm the scoundrel I'm often painted and this is also true of Quentin. In many ways he is likable and a very decent sort. But he has a streak of wildness which seems to get him in continual trouble."

"Why should he come here posing as David Cartill?"

"He daren't come back here as himself."

"Why?"

Barnabas looked away. "He has gotten himself in fairly serious trouble here. He has been asked to leave by the family. So he manages to get back by assuming a new personality and a disguise. Yet I know him so well I could see through his fagade at once."

"Roger Collins couldn't have, since he rented the cottage to him and his supposed wife."

Barnabas smiled grimly. "Roger doesn't know him all that well, though he unquestionably has heard his history. I don't think Quentin would have too much trouble fooling him or the others."

"And you feel reasonably sure Cartill is Quentin?"

"Yes."

"And the dark girl he calls his wife?"

"An accomplice. Someone he has met along the way." She frowned. "Why should he come here and try to hold us up with the treasure hunt?"

"Malice. He'd enjoy annoying Roger."

"Do you think there are a real David and Belle Cartill?"

"Probably. He's just assumed their identity for his visit here."

"He claims she's interested in voodoo."

"That could be."

"And she's supposed to be the direct descendant of Jenny Swift."

"That also could be, though I doubt it. I'd say it's just another mad prank of Quentin's to bother everyone. He's done things like this before."

Norah stared at the handsome man. "What sort of trouble was Quentin in?"

He waited a moment before replying. Then very slowly he said, "It is rather complicated. Some people believe he was cursed. They say that under a certain full moon he takes on wolf-like attributes. He has been called the wolf man and accused of some violent crimes. Of course none of it has been proven. But the family feels better with him out of the way."

"I can well understand that," she said, stunned. "What do you think about the stories?"

"There are some foundations of truth in the rumors," he admitted. "That is why you could have been in some danger tonight. He might have slipped into his werewolf personality if I hadn't happened to come along."

"That's fantastic!"

"Most things about Quentin are," he said. "If you keep it in mind you'll be able to cope with him much better."

She sat in her chair limply. "At last I'm beginning to discover the truth about Collinwood. It isn't what it seemed to be at first, so quiet and pleasant."

"Far from it," Barnabas said grimly.

"What can we do about Quentin? Shall I tell my father and the others that David Cartill and his wife are imposters?"

"No, that wouldn't be wise—not until I can think of some way to prove it."

She looked unhappy. "So I won't be able to say anything?"

"I'm afraid not."

"I don't like that."

Barnabas said, "I wouldn't worry about it. As I've explained, Quentin isn't all that wicked a character, though I don't know about the girl. She could be a bad influence on him."

Norah frowned. "She behaved rather strangely, now that I remember. All during the time we talked she kept silent. It was David—or Quentin—who did all the talking. She was quiet and rather sinister."

"Probably she'll bear watching."

She gave him an earnest, questioning glance. "Do you believe in all this ghost talk? That the evil spirit of Jenny Swift may try to prevent us from recovering the treasure? You sounded like it last night."

His face became solemn. "Collinwood is a place of phantoms. Jenny Swift's could well be one of them."

"Perhaps we should never have come here at all," she worried.

"It's too late to think about that now. You are committed to searching for the treasure."

"Yes. I wish you were around more in the daylight hours," she fretted. "Then you would be able to help us."

"I appreciate your confidence," Barnabas said. "But you'd better remember that I am also under suspicion."

"That's ridiculous."

His deep-set eyes met hers. "You must have already heard some things about me. I mean unflattering things."

She looked down. "The worst I've heard is to have your name linked with your ancestor. Some of the local people apparently feel the vampire taint has gone on down through the years, and that you also suffer from the curse of the living dead."

"You see," he said lightly,

Norah glanced up at him again. "I don't believe it."

"Thank you."

"But I suppose even I have been influenced by hearing the story," she was forced to admit. "I mentioned the weird dream I had when you came to me in the night and kissed me on the throat."

"Yes, you did," he said in an odd, dry voice.

"Probably that was brought on by my hearing those vampire stories," she said. "And it's lodged in my subconscious, for the dream has been repeated."

"I'm sorry to intrude in your nightmares," Barnabas said with some irony.

"Please don't be angry that I've brought it up again."

"Not at all."

"It's that maid, Lucy. She kept filling me with weird stories of the supernatural which she claimed she'd heard from her father."

"The villagers are superstitious," Barnabas agreed. "But I have an idea that your bringing this up and discussing it so fully this time may have a beneficial effect."

"In what way?"

He eyed her sharply. "I don't think you're going to have the dream again."

She was startled by the certainty with which he said this. "Do you really believe that?"

"I do."

She smiled wanly. "With all my other problems, I can't think that it is very important."

"I'd like to see your mind at rest."

"At least one good thing has happened to me here," she said, rising and looking at him with gentle eyes. "I have found you. My father has often teased me about not being able to find a man whom I could really respect and care for. That isn't true any longer."

Barnabas' gaunt face brightened. "Norah!" he said with deep emotion.

"I may as well be honest," she said. "My mind isn't on the treasure hunt as it should be. I'm in a confused mood. I've fallen in love with you, Barnabas."

"Dear Norah!" He drew her to him and pressed his lips to hers.

That his lips were ice cold mattered not at all. She didn't even think of it as she relaxed in the shelter of his strong embrace. She felt this was where she belonged and she wanted to remain with him forever.

When he at last released her, she asked, "Would you be willing to give up this life you're living? Could you consider sacrificing your freedom to marry me?"

His eyes were sad. "Dear Norah, it's impossible for me to

explain. But at this moment I don't see that it could ever be. As much as I love you, I'll never be free to share my life with you."

Despair replaced hope. Her eyes moistened. "There is someone else?"

"No one," he said. "Rather it is the role life has cast for me. I'm in iron fetters from which I may never escape."

"Can't I even hope?"

He smiled sadly. "Let us not deny ourselves that small luxury," he said. "We can hope that events may change. In the meantime we must be content in remaining the best of friends."

Her pretty face was baffled. "Collinwood is truly a place of mysteries. There is so much here I don't understand."

"Then consider yourself fortunate," was his reply. "And now I must see you safely back."

She made no protest. Still feeling depressed, she allowed him to escort her back to the main door of Collinwood. There in the darkness he kissed her tenderly again and said goodnight. She watched as he walked away into the shadows and then she went inside.

Carolyn was standing there in the entrance hall in a silk dressing gown. She said, "You're late getting back. I'm the only one up."

Somewhat flustered, she said, "The night passed quickly."

The old house was very silent except for the ticking of the old grandfather's clock in the hallway. The lights were out in the living room; the hall and stairway were shadowed.

Carolyn gave her a knowing look. "I saw you just now. I didn't mean to spy. I heard voices and looked out. I couldn't help it."

"Oh?" she replied nervously.

"Barnabas was kissing you," Carolyn said. "I'm sure you must have been warned about becoming too friendly with him."

"I like Barnabas," she said defiantly.

"So do I," Carolyn said at once. "But there are certain things which can't be ignored. You must know that Julia Hoffman is in love with him and that for a while she had him under treatment at her clinic."

"Dr. Hoffman mentioned that to me tonight," Norah said. "She was very mysterious about it."

Carolyn nodded solemnly. "I have an idea she saw a romance developing between you and Barnabas. She was warning you off."

"What right has she?"

"I suppose none," Carolyn admitted. "I'm sure Barnabas doesn't return her love. But still you might be wise to listen to her."

"A jealous woman?"

"But a doctor."

Norah frowned. "What did she treat Barnabas for?"

"I don't think I have the right to talk about that," Carolyn replied. "But he left the clinic before he was cured. I can tell you that much."

"So he is not in good health?"

"Not in normal health," was Carolyn's careful reply.

"Thanks for telling me," she said. "I know nothing may come of my caring for Barnabas. But I can't help it and I'm not ashamed."

Carolyn sighed. "I was afraid you'd say something like that. I'll never talk to you about it again unless you bring it up. I don't want to interfere in any way."

Norah offered her a friendly smile. "I'm sure of that And now I'll say goodnight."

"Goodnight," Carolyn called after her wistfully as she started up the stairs.

As she prepared for bed, she decided that it was easy to understand why Barnabas would not consider marriage. He was aware of his bad health and not ready to ask a wife to share his problem. She would be perfectly willing to take the risk, but knowing how unselfish Barnabas was, she despaired of convincing him this would be the wise course.

Sleep, when it came, was restless and disturbed. She had gruesome dreams in which macabre faces pressed close to hers. She stood on the wharf to see the vessel *Jenny Swift* tossed on turbulent waves. Battered by the storm, the masts toppled. Finally the ancient vessel rolled over on its side and sank beneath the monstrous, angry waves.

Then the pirate queen came up out of the water to stand on the wharf in the raging storm staring at her. At first Norah saw only the lovely side of the phantom's face; then the mutilated other side was revealed to her and she screamed. All went blank and she was wandering in a cemetery. Voices were whispering to her, trying to attract her attention. The voices of the dead buried beneath her.

But in all the swiftly changing scenes of her nightmare there was no Barnabas. The weird scene in which he came to her bedside and kissed her did not take place. When she opened her eyes to the gray morning she knew that the familiar dream had not been repeated. Barnabas had been right in his theory about that.

Lucy brought in her breakfast tray with the air of one who had momentous news. As Norah sat down to have breakfast, the maid told her, "There was a lot of excitement in the village last night."

"Indeed?" She looked up at the stout girl's tense face.

"Yes, miss," Lucy informed her. "One of the waitresses at the Blue Whale was attacked on her way home."

"Attacked?"

"Yes, miss. Some neighbors saw her wandering near her house and went out to her. She was in a kind of faint, her clothes were torn, and she had a funny red mark on her throat as if she'd been bitten."

The girl's words made her start. "A red mark on her throat!"

"Yes, miss," the maid said. "She didn't seem to remember anything. It's like what happened here a year or two ago."

"A year or two ago?"

"Yes, miss. Then there were a number of attacks on girls in the village. It went on all through the summer and fall. There was a real stir about it. The newspapers had stories telling about the monster in black. That's how they described whoever it was."

"Did they catch him?"

"No," Lucy said with a worried air. "Now it seems like he's come back to do it all over again."

"And they have no idea who it is?"

Lucy looked wary. "I guess maybe the police have an idea, miss. But I wouldn't want to guess." And with that she went out.

When Norah went downstairs, her father notified her that the tug had arrived with the bathysphere and she was caught up in the excitement of getting the project under way. Forgetting Lucy's "monster in black," she went down to the wharf with her father and saw the bathysphere and the tug were tied to one side of it while the scow was at the other. A half-dozen of the crew were at work and there were some spectators on the wharf and along the beach.

Her father led her directly to the place where the bathysphere awaited them and addressed himself to a pleasant, ruddy-faced man. "Glad to see you, Captain."

"Glad to be here, sir," the young man said, touching his battered peaked cap. "There was no excitement on the way down."

Claude Bliss said, "I want you to meet my daughter, Norah. This is our new captain, Jim Donovan."

"You've joined us at an especially difficult time," she told him. "The treasure of *The Jenny Swift* seems to have eluded all the other salvage expeditions."

Captain Donovan gestured toward the bathysphere with his straight-stemmed pipe and said, "None of them had a diving bell like this. We'll really be able to work down below."

"That's so," she agreed.

"There have been some other problems," her father said grimly, and she knew he was referring to the claims of David and Belle Cartill, "but they are no concern of yours."

The young captain seemed enthusiastic. "If it's all right with you, sir," he said, "I'd like to move out to the water directly over the wreck and make some tests today."

"No reason why you shouldn't," her father said. "I'll want to make the first trip down in the bathysphere."

Norah asked, "May I go along?"

Her father hesitated, then said, "I suppose it might be a good time for you to do it. We'll not be engaged in any practical work. Later there'll be no room for you. We must give all the space to our divers."

"If I'm to help in directing from the tug I should have some picture of what it's like below."

"No question of that," Captain Donovan said with a friendly smile on his rather plain face. "Can you be ready to go in a half-hour, miss?"

"Whenever my father is ready, I'll be able to join him." Less than thirty minutes later she, her father and Jim Donovan descended into the diving bell with its three- and-a-half-foot metal walls. Inside there was less room than she'd expected. The intricate mechanism took a lot of the space and there was also the escape and entry chamber for when the divers used the sphere as their headquarters.

She had a tiny pang of fear as the top of the diving bell was put in place and locked. Then there was a murmuring of the complicated machinery all around her. They were at once on the special air system which had been installed in the sphere. While her father and Captain Donovan discussed the function of various controls, she stood by having no sensation of the bell being lowered into the depths of the deep cove.

She asked, "Are we under way now?"

The young captain smiled at her. "We have been for several minutes."

"Turn on the spotlights," her father suggested.

The captain went over to a bank of switches and as he manipulated them the watery world outside began to light up. They were down almost to the bottom, she realized with some surprise. The greenish water was murky and light resistant. They were in the weird depths which had been the grave of so many vessels and their crews.

"It's a strange world," she gasped as she stared out the thick glass windows. "Being in here gives you a different sensation from diving in a suit or just skin diving. You get such a remote view of things."

Her father nodded. "This way the two worlds are apart." And to the young man at the controls, he said, "If your markings were correct, Captain, we should be close to *The Jenny Swift* by now."

"In a moment," Jim Donovan said, his eyes on the instruments.

There was a slight bump as the sphere came to the bottom

of the cove. Norah steadied herself. "We must be at the end of our journey."

"Yes," the young captain agreed.

Her father was at the observation window peering out into the underwater world. All at once, he cried, "Look! Over there!"

She glanced out and after a few seconds was able to discern the hull of an ancient vessel resting on its side, half-submerged in sand. Fish swam over it and around it. It was a first for Norah. She'd walked in the ocean depths and crawled over the hulls of sunken craft. But never before had she sat in a dry room under the ocean and looked out at a wrecked vessel. No doubt within that silent hull in the murky green water the skeletons of the crew still kept a ghostly vigil. The thought of it sent a chill down her spine.

"It's a macabre world," she said in an awed voice. "I wonder why we dare to venture into it."

Her father gave her a disapproving glance. "I hope you're not going to allow talk of the curse to bother you."

"No," she said, but without conviction.

Donovan smiled at her. "This diving bell opens up all kinds of new doors for us," he said. "We'll get down to the salvage work in half the time we would using a straight diving operation."

"I suppose so."

"We know we have the location correct," Donovan told her father. "Will we signal to be taken back up?"

"We might as well," Claude Bliss said, his thin face wearing a look of elation. "Tomorrow we'll begin the real work."

The young captain spoke into an intercom and in a few minutes they began the ascent. Not until Norah was assisted out onto the deck did she feel really at ease. It had been a strange and terrifying experience, even for one as experienced in underwater exploration as herself.

Her father seemed well satisfied and the tug moved in to the wharf once more. At least thirty or forty spectators were lined along the beach watching it all. She gave her father a grim smile. "We seem to be attracting a lot of attention."

"We've had a lot of publicity," Claude Bliss said. "Wait until we start fetching up that gold bullion."

When the tug bumped against the wharf, one of the crew came forward to help lift her up onto the weathered logs. She smiled and rested her weight on him as she scrambled from the tug to the wharf. She had one foot on the wharf when the tug gave a sudden lurch, knocking her off balance. With a cry of terror she toppled down between tug and wharf into the water. As she struggled to the surface, coughing, the tug swayed back and struck her head. Pain exploded like fireworks behind her eyes, and she blacked out!

CHAPTER 6

It must have been only a matter of minutes later that Norah opened her eyes to find herself stretched out, wet and miserable, on the wharf. Her father and Captain Donovan were bending over her with troubled faces. As awareness returned to her, she was conscious of other faces looking down at her curiously.

Her father said, "Thank Heaven you're all right!"

Staring at him, she murmured, "My head aches!"

"No reason why it shouldn't," he said. "You received a nasty blow when the tug swung back in."

Donovan said fiercely, "It was sloppy seamanship on someone's part. I'll get to the bottom of it."

"Don't blame anyone," she protested weakly. "It was me. When the tug moved I lost my balance." And she saw that he was as soaking wet as herself. "You jumped in after me?"

"It was as little as I could do."

She raised herself up, embarrassed at being stared at by the others who had gathered round. To her father, she said, "I can walk nicely. Get me away from here. I dislike being the seaside attraction."

"Sure you're not too weak?" her father worried as he assisted her to her feet.

"Not at all," she said, avoiding the faces of the strangers on the wharf.

But as she turned to leave, Carson Blythe confronted her agitatedly.

"I hope what happened just now will make you realize how potent the curse is," he said.

"I lost my balance, Mr. Blythe," she said firmly, annoyed at her way of escape being blocked by the frail, white-haired man. "It had nothing at all to do with the curse."

"You are wrong, Miss Bliss. You have been given a warning. Be wise enough to take it."

"Please, Mr. Blythe," she said wearily.

"My daughter is anxious to get away from here," her father was forced to explain.

Carson Blythe shrugged and stepped aside. "I can see how this is beginning. Your luck will be no better than mine."

When they were out of earshot, Norah said angrily, "How thoughtless of him to hinder me like that when he saw what a state I was in!"

"He seems a very strange person," Donovan observed. "What is all this curse talk I'm hearing?"

Her father explained, "It has to do with the bad luck Blythe experienced at the time he was trying to bring up the treasure from *The Jenny Swift*."

"I see."

"His wife killed herself and a storm lost him all his equipment and any chance of completing the salvage operation," her father said. "Since then he's become a bitter, twisted person."

"He must have always been weak," Norah decided, "or he wouldn't have allowed himself to be broken in this manner."

They reached the top of the cliff and the walk across the lawns to Collinwood was a short one. There Elizabeth received her with shock and distress. She was at once sent up to her bedroom for a hot bath and a warm drink following it. Then Norah relaxed in bed.

Elizabeth hovered at her bedside like a nervous mother hen. "You're sure you won't let me call a doctor?"

"No," she said. "I don't need one. I'm feeling ever so much better."

"Still, you can't tell."

"I'll be fine," Norah assured her.

After Elizabeth left, she closed her eyes and rested for a little, but she couldn't sleep. Just remaining in bed became boring, so she got up and put on her dressing gown. Her head had a sore spot and she felt a bit dizzy when she moved too quickly, but she was sure she'd suffered no serious injury.

The day continued to be sunless. She went to the window and stared out. She could see the wharf and noted that there was plenty of activity around it. Preparations were under way for the real work which would begin tomorrow if the weather were right. She felt angry with herself for having been so clumsy, but she refused to think it had anything to do with Jenny's curse.

After a while she dressed and went out for a stroll. Elizabeth was nowhere in sight and neither was Carolyn, so she was able to escape safely from the mansion.

She started out across the lawn in the direction away from the wharf. She knew there was no use in going to call on Barnabas; Willie Loomis would refuse to let her see him. She'd have to wait until dusk to tell him all the news.

She strolled along slowly and before she knew it she had come to the yard of the cottage the Cartills were renting. She saw Belle Cartill's swarthy, pretty face appear at a rear window of the cottage and study her briefly. Then the girl vanished.

A moment later, before Norah had a chance to continue on along the path, a door opened and David Cartill —or Quentin Collins— emerged. He wore a short-sleeved shirt open at the neck.

"Hello," he called out with a smile. "Have you come for a visit?"

"Do you think that's likely?" She responded coldly.

He came down the cottage steps to stand nearer her. "You never can tell," he said. His shrewd eyes were sizing her up.

"You ran off quickly last night when Barnabas arrived," she said.

"Was that who that was?"

"Don't pretend you don't know him."

"I don't," he said with a winning innocence. "You forget I'm a stranger here."

"Opinions may vary on that."

He lifted his eyebrows. "Now what on earth do you mean?"

She eyed him defiantly. "Have you ever heard of Quentin Collins?"

"What a pleasant name."

"Does it sound familiar to you?"

"I like it," he said. "But I don't know it."

"I think you should."

"Indeed? Well, then, I must rack my brain, mustn't I?"

"Barnabas is on to your tricks," she told him.

"Barnabas is?" The young man looked baffled. "Now what does that mean?"

"I think you know."

"I swear you talk in nothing but riddles."

Norah said, "And I suppose you expect us to believe that the young woman I just saw in the window is your wife?"

"And why not?"

"Because you have no wife."

He looked shocked. "Well, I trust Belle never hears you talking about her like that. I can show you our marriage certificate from the island."

"Then she has to be Mrs. Quentin Collins."

"Nothing of the sort," he said stoutly. "I can't imagine where you got on to this name of Quentin Collins or what it has to do with my wife and me. And I thought you had come to inform me you'd decided to make a deal about the treasure."

"Not likely."

"Fight it out in the courts if you wish," he said. "As I told you, I'm a lawyer and can act for us. My wife is a direct descendant of that lady pirate and we have the papers to prove it."

"You can discuss that with my father."

"I shall, don't doubt it," he said. "And you tell your arrogant friend, Barnabas, that I'll thank him not to confuse me with someone else."

"He'll be interested in your comments, I promise you," she said.

His eyes twinkled. "I hardly expected to see you after your near drowning."

She frowned. "You heard?"

"That sort of news travels fast in a village. People are saying you suffered from *The Jenny Swift* curse."

"That's a lot of nonsense."

"Well," the young man sighed, "no one can accuse you of being easy to convince about anything. It makes me feel bad to think of dragging your father and you along with the righteous Roger Collins into the courts for a share of what is rightly my wife's."

"It's all a trick on your part to torment Roger," she accused him.

"I'd hardly come all the way from Barbados to waste my time on a prank," he protested.

"We'll see about that." She turned and started back along the path toward Collinwood again.

He shouted after her, "Sure you won't join Belle and me for a cup of tea?"

She glanced back over her shoulder with a derisive smile. "Hardly, not after her being out all night collecting voodoo herbs."

He chuckled. "You remembered!"

"I'm not forgetting anything you say," she warned him and then continued on her way without looking back.

There had been a bantering air in his manner which made her almost sure Barnabas had been right about him—this was the renegade Quentin Collins back playing tricks on his pretentious relatives. All his arguments had been offered lightly and he didn't seem really concerned about his wife's supposed share of the sunken treasure.

Her meeting with him would be another thing to tell Barnabas in the evening. She gave a deep sigh at the thought that it would be hours before she'd have the opportunity to talk to the man she loved again.

There was no doubt in her mind that she did love him. Regardless of what the others might think or say, she was certain she could be happy with him.

As she reached Collinwood she was surprised to see Professor Stokes standing in the garden. She at once went up to him. He looked surprised.

"Mrs. Stoddard told us you were in your room resting after your accident," he said.

She smiled. "No. I felt so much better I decided on a walk."

The professor looked grave. "You might have easily been drowned if that young man hadn't plunged in at once and rescued you."

"I suppose that's true," she acknowledged.

"You could have sunk between the tug and dock and not been located until it was too late."

"Captain Donovan lost no time coming to my aid," she said.

"Very commendable," the professor said, "though not a very good omen for the beginning of our mutual enterprise. It seems there may be something to that curse."

"Surely you should be the last to say that," she reproached him. "You were strong in your denials when Barnabas suggested exactly the same thing."

The portly man looked embarrassed. "I'm not changing my tune," he protested. "But I don't like the way things are shaping up. You've heard, of course, of the claim this wretched David Cartill and his wife propose to make against our enterprise."

"I wouldn't let that worry me too much either."

Professor Stokes raised his eyebrows. "Why on earth not? The man is talking about making us give him half the treasure findings! Don't you consider that a serious matter?"

"Only if he can prove his claims," she said, regretting that she couldn't share her full knowledge with him. But Barnabas had warned her to make no mention of Quentin. "And until a final report comes in from our lawyers, we're only guessing."

He nodded. "That's true."

"Is Dr. Hoffman here?" she asked, wondering if she'd made the journey with him.

Professor Stokes looked suddenly uneasy. Clearing his throat, he said, "I believe she has gone to visit Barnabas." She stared at him with surprise. "Barnabas sees no one in the daytime."

"He was under her medical care," the professor said. "It is possible he may make an exception because of that."

"Possibly," she said quietly.

"We have talked with your father and seen the diving bell. I'm very much impressed by it and in spite of this rather bad beginning I still have the highest hopes." It was plainly an attempt to change the subject.

"Where is father?"

"Still at the wharf," the professor said. "There is a great deal to be done and he likes to supervise all the details."

"I know," she said, guiltily. "I should be helping. I would be if I hadn't been so stupid getting off the tug."

"You shouldn't blame yourself. Accidents happen to us all."

"I suppose so," she said dully. "Will you excuse me, Professor? I'm feeling rather weary suddenly."

"Certainly," he said in his hearty fashion. "Take care of yourself. You're needed for the success of our venture."

She moved on toward the side entrance of Collinwood, but she didn't go in. Instead she went on around the mansion and past the parking area and the stables. She was taking the most direct route to the old house. Would Barnabas really see Julia Hoffman in the daylight hours but not her? She felt hurt and perhaps even jealous. What was the hold Julia had over Barnabas?

As she approached the red brick house with its locked shutters she had some misgivings. Perhaps the professor had been wrong. Dr. Hoffman might have gone somewhere else. But having come this far, she didn't feel like turning back.

Instead of approaching the front entrance, she went on around to the back of the house where there was a bulkhead. And her intuition paid off. The cover of the bulkhead was swung back to reveal moss-covered stone steps leading to the cellar. She felt reasonably certain that if Julia Hoffman were in the house, this was how she'd entered.

Cautiously she descended the steps one at a time until she came to the open door leading into the pitch-black cellar itself. She edged forward into the damp and darkness. After she'd taken a few steps inside, her eyes became more accustomed to the murky atmosphere and she spied a doorway at the right. A pale glow of light was coming from it.

She groped her way in the darkness until she was only a few steps from the doorway. At that moment Julia Hoffman came out of the hidden room to stand framed in the doorway facing her.

The doctor gasped. "What are you doing down here?"

Norah raised her chin defiantly. "I heard you'd come to see Barnabas and I followed you."

"You had no right!" Julia said with shock in her tone. "Why not? I'm very fond of Barnabas."

Julia came closer to her, looking bitter and angry. "You poor young fool! You should know better!"

"What do you mean?"

"Barnabas is a very sick man. If you had any consideration for him you would not want to intrude on him when he is resting."

She hesitated. "Is he resting in there?"

"Yes."

"You intruded on him," Norah reminded her.

Julia Hoffman made a despairing gesture. "I went in there to see him as a doctor, to give him any help I could. Not as a lovesick young idiot."

Norah wavered. "If Barnabas is all that ill I want to be with him."

The older woman still stood in her way. "He is asleep. He needs sleep very badly. If you go in there now you'll regret it."

"But it's so gloomy and awful down here," she protested. "Why would he choose such a place to come if he's ill?"

"More stupid questions," Julia Hoffman replied in a strained voice. "He came down here because it was especially quiet and he needs seclusion when he is like this."

She stared at the woman doctor with troubled eyes. "How can I believe you?"

"Because you know I love him just as you do," Julia said earnestly. "And unless his health is improved my love is just as helpless as yours. Please do as I ask. Leave here with me. By this evening Barnabas may be himself again."

Norah still hesitated, wanting to see for herself despite Julia's obvious sincerity. But she would be seeing Barnabas in a few hours at the most and she could talk to him about this then.

Quietly, she said, "Very well. I'll do as you say."

Julia Hoffman's face showed relief. "You won't regret it."

The doctor took her by the arm and they went back along the dark cellar to the steps which led to the bulkhead and outside. They mounted the steps and were in the open air once more.

Julia swung the bulkhead door back in place. "I didn't want Willie Loomis to know I was here," she said. "I think he's left the house for a little, to see the diving bell. Half the village is there."

Norah was still tense and worried. "Barnabas will be all right?" she asked.

"Yes," Julia said. "Don't worry about it. He has been as ill as this many times before."

She stared at the older woman. "Why didn't he continue his treatments with you?"

"That is a long story." The woman sighed. "I haven't time to tell you now."

"I'll talk to him about it," Norah suggested. "Perhaps he'll agree to go back to your clinic."

Julia smiled sadly. "I wish it could be as simple as that. I don't object to you discussing it with him, but I predict you'll have no luck. You understand so little about Barnabas."

"I'm going to be an influence in his life," Norah said defiantly. "I'm going to change him. And one day we'll be married."

The older woman shrugged. "That might be good for both of you.

It has a familiar ring to me—it sounds like my own dreams. I hope yours aren't shattered so easily." "I don't intend they shall be."

"My dear," the doctor said, "Barnabas has lived a very long while, and during that time many women have fallen in love with him. Not by his wish, since he lost his heart long ago to someone who has been dead for years. He has left a trail of broken hearts after him, including mine. I would wish that you'd see the danger and try not to be serious about him."

"You want him for yourself!"

"That will never be. Nor are you likely to win him. Why not turn to the young hero of today? The captain who saved your life."

"I happen to love Barnabas."

Julia nodded sadly. "A common complaint. And I'm afraid he must be the one to cure you of it."

"I'll tell him what you said," Norah promised.

"By all means do that," Dr. Julia Hoffman told her. "Barnabas knows my feelings. And now I must go back to Collinwood and join Professor Stokes. It is imperative that we return to the clinic this evening. I have several patients who require close attention."

Norah walked back to Collinwood with her in silence. There was nothing more to be said between them. For her part, Norah felt spent and unhappy. It seemed to her that much of what was happening and being said around her was lost on her because she did not fully understand the situation. Tonight she would query Barnabas more directly about himself.

Professor Stokes looked relieved when they came up to him. "Ah, so you've found each other. I was worried."

Dr. Hoffman gave him a sardonic glance. "I assume you told Norah where to look for me?"

He looked embarrassed. "Why, yes, I guess I did."

"I thought so," she said with a sigh. And to Norah, "Goodbye, my dear. I want you to remember what I've told you."

Professor Stokes smiled at her nervously. "Good luck with the salvage work when you begin tomorrow, Miss Bliss." And then the two left her to go to their car.

She went inside and upstairs to change for dinner, wondering what would have happened if she'd simply pushed past Julia Hoffman and gone on in to Barnabas. It was unlikely she'd ever manage to enter the house in daytime again; Willie Loomis kept it guarded too well.

When she went downstairs to join the others Roger Collins was addressing her father and the members of his family in a serious vein. He halted his talk to turn to her with his cocktail glass in hand and say, "I'm glad you're feeling well enough to join us, Miss Bliss."

"I'm fine now," she assured him.

"Good," he said. "I have just been telling the others that we are faced with an unpleasant situation here at Collinwood. I mean aside from the trouble we're having with this David Cartill character and his wife."

"Oh?" she said.

"Yes," Roger went on. "The treasure hunt has drawn a great many idle and curious people to the estate. It's going to be difficult to cope with them."

Her father spoke up. "Aren't they technically trespassers? Couldn't your men keep them from using the estate road to reach the wharf?"

Roger Collins nodded. "They could. But they can still find their way to the wharf by walking along the beach, and the beach happens to be public property."

"It's awkward," Elizabeth Stoddard commented. "By keeping them from the road we'd only increase their hostility and they'd swarm down on the wharf just the same."

"I see," Norah's father said with a frown. "You are right. It is terribly awkward."

"I'm afraid we'll just have to put up with some nuisance until the novelty wears off," Roger Collins said. "And we can hope that will happen soon."

Claude Bliss suggested, "Perhaps when we move out on the cove they'll not have so much to watch."

"When Carson Blythe was making his salvage attempts they often went out in small boats and clustered around his barge," Carolyn said. "I remember."

"Treasure hunts have a peculiar fascination for most people, I fear," was her mother's comment.

Roger paused and frowned. "Now there is another matter."

"Must it be discussed here?" Elizabeth asked.

"I fear so. It is only right we be fair to our guests. The rest of you know only too well what I'm talking about."

Carolyn looked unhappy. "You're making a lot of fuss about very little. Uncle Roger."

"Let me be the judge of that," Roger said crisply.

Norah's father looked around with a hint of embarrassment. "I trust we are not intruding on a family matter."

"Hardly," Roger said so coldly that Norah felt a sudden rush of fear. She was almost certain this was going to be unpleasant—and about Barnabas. She waited tensely.

Elizabeth looked pale. "I agree with Carolyn," she said. "You are allowing yourself to become much too upset."

"I have reason to be upset," Roger said, his face deathly pale. He turned to Norah and her father. "Today I had the unpleasant experience of being questioned by the state police at length about a young woman who was attacked in the village last night. She was found dazed and weak, with an odd red mark on her throat."

"What about the mark?" Norah asked in a voice that was close to a whisper.

Roger looked at her queerly. "The mark was the clue. Several years ago similar attacks were made on village girls. It became a scandal. And the police traced them to our cousin Barnabas."

Carolyn cried out, "Nothing was proven!"

"Because I spoke to Barnabas and had him leave here before the police could go into the thing any further. This has happened several times in the past And now it looks as if Barnabas is in trouble again."

Norah was staring at the stern face of Roger Collins with dismay. "Why should Barnabas be blamed?"

"Because," Roger Collins said coldly, "it appears he suffers from a strange madness which makes him believe he is the reincarnation of the first Barnabas Collins. The Barnabas Collins who bit into young women's throats for their blood. Who was banished from the village as a vampire!"

CHAPTER 7

It was Carolyn who spoke up indignantly. "I don't think you are being at all fair, Uncle Roger. You're offering us your theory rather than fact. You have no right to suggest Barnabas is mentally unsound!"

Norah felt like applauding, but she knew as a guest she had to keep strictly out of this family argument. She would find some other way to champion Barnabas when the right moment came.

Elizabeth Stoddard, looking pale, said, "Carolyn, you are just as wrong to condemn your uncle. We all know that Barnabas is"—she paused and looked covertly at Norah—"that he was treated by Dr. Hoffman."

"Exactly," Roger Collins said in his stem fashion. "I don't think it is a matter of arguing about whether what I have said is true or not, but rather to decide what we, as a family, are going to do about the unhappy business." Elizabeth sighed. "It seems clear enough. You'll have to ask Barnabas to leave Collinwood. At least then we're not in any way responsible."

"The old house was left for his use," Carolyn pointed out. "You can't put him out of it."

Roger frowned ather. "I can at least suggest for the good of all he leave. And I can tell him it is the wish of the family that he do so."

"Not my wish!" Carolyn protested.

Roger looked at Norah and her father apologetically. "Forgive me for bringing this matter up, but you had to know. Better you hear it from us than from some of the villagers."

Norah's father said, "I hope none of this can be blamed on our treasure hunt. I regret we've brought so many curiosity seekers here. I had no idea it would happen."

"This is an old business," Elizabeth said wearily. "You are in no way responsible."

"Though when people do group around together idly, they gossip more," Roger said. "And the treasure hunt has, as I've pointed out, brought a lot of idle people to the beach."

"Surely the excitement will dwindle," Claude Bliss said.

"I trust so," Roger replied. "I will make it a point to speak with Barnabas at the earliest and try and persuade him to leave."

This discussion had dampened everyone's spirits; there was little conversation at the dinner table. Norah was tormented with worry for Barnabas. All she could think of was getting away from the group and warning him what they meant to confront him with. This would mean again going out into the darkness alone, which Barnabas had warned her against, but in spite of her good resolutions it appeared she had little choice. She had to let him know about the wave of resentment growing against him in the old mansion.

The talk at the table turned to the other situation bothering Roger and the rest of them.

"Was that David Cartill on the beach to observe today?" Roger asked her father.

Claude looked bleak. "I'm afraid he was. He came to me and asked if we'd had any meeting to consider his requests."

"What did you tell him?"

"That we had no intention of tolerating either him or his demands."

"Excellent." Roger Collins nodded his appreciation. "There is something unpleasantly familiar about that fellow. Several times today he came into my mind and I tried to place where I may have seen him before, but I had no success."

Norah listened with hidden excitement. Perhaps the spotlight would turn to Quentin and from Barnabas. Rather recklessly she said, "I heard the name of Quentin Collins mentioned by someone on the beach today. Who is he?"

She might just as well have tossed a bomb into their midst. There was general consternation at the table though no one spoke for a moment. She saw her father glare at her with disapproval and deliberately avoided his eye.

Roger Collins' sharp eyes were probing as he demanded, "Who did you hear speak of Quentin Collins?"

"I don't know," she said, pretending innocence. "The name just came to me from someone in the crowd. I think they said something about where is Quentin with all this going on?"

Elizabeth gave her brother a stricken glance. "You see! The villagers have long memories!"

"It's good to know they gossip about someone besides Barnabas," Carolyn said with relish.

Norah thought she'd been successful enough to push her game a little further. "You all seem so upset! Was it wrong of me to mention the name? If so, I'm sorry."

Roger Collins stared suspiciously at her for a moment, then said, "Quentin Collins is a member of another branch of the Collins family. Like Barnabas, he has paid several visits here."

"Like Barnabas?" she echoed, turning it into a question.

Elizabeth spoke up from her end of the table. "Quentin is another young man not held in esteem by the family. Every time he has come here he has caused trouble."

"Does he also resemble Barnabas in appearance?" she asked. This was her trump card. Surely it would make someone in the group recognize whom David Cartill so resembled.

"He doesn't look anything like Barnabas," Carolyn answered. "But he is good-looking, with wavy hair and sideburns." She halted, as if a surprising thought had just struck her. "In fact, if it weren't for the goatee, I'd say David Cartill is almost a look-alike for him."

"Oh, you're wrong, Carolyn," her mother protested. "I'm sure Quentin is a much taller man than that Cartill."

Roger Collins was frowning. "There is a resemblance. Perhaps that is what was bothering me today and I couldn't place the likeness. Yes, it could very well be."

Carolyn gave Norah a warm smile. "At least that gives you a general picture of what Quentin looks like. He hasn't been here for some time and so I suppose most of us have forgotten about him."

"Yet somebody on the beach remembered him," Elizabeth worried. "If they hadn't they wouldn't have brought up his name."

Norah was content to let the conversation turn to something else. She had brought Quentin's name up, that was enough for at least a little while. She had an idea she might have planted a suspicion as to the real identity of David Cartill in Roger's mind, though he hadn't indicated any concern in this direction. This didn't mean too much, as the stern head of the Collins clan was not one to easily reveal his thoughts.

Dinner ended and she became more uneasy and determined to slip away from the others. She moved to the window and saw that it was nearing dusk. While she stood there staring out, her father came to her. In a low voice he said, "I was shocked by your stupid behavior at dinner."

She looked at him in surprise. Not often had he sounded so upset. She said, "Good grief, all I did was ask a simple question."

"You had no right to mention Quentin Collins. The family are worried enough about Barnabas."

"They are being unfair to Barnabas," she said with some anger.

"We're not in a position to offer judgments," her father reminded her sharply. "We are guests in this house."

"The way things are shaping up, I'd prefer not to be."

Claude Bliss looked pale and tired. "We are not getting off to a very good start as things are. Why try to make the situation worse?"

"I merely repeated a name I heard."

"It is unfortunate that the name of Quentin Collins is not a popular one with the family," her father said. "He has caused them almost as much annoyance as Barnabas."

"How could I know that?"

"I'm telling you now," her father said. "Please, don't speak of him again under any circumstances."

She gave her parent a concerned look. "But Carolyn claims this David Cartill greatly resembles Quentin. Suppose he is Quentin in disguise?"

Her father shook his head. "That is most unlikely."

"How can you be certain?"

"It's not our big problem at the moment," her father told her. "My lawyers will have full information on the Cartills shortly. We must just wait until then. And I'll depend on you not to continue your friendship with this Barnabas."

"It's not fair of you to ask that," she protested. "You've heard something of his reputation, isn't that enough?"

"I think much of it is exaggerated."

"Again I suspect you're wrong," Claude Bliss warned her. "At least, I'll depend on you to think before you speak in the future. I count on you to be tactful."

Roger Collins fortunately came to take him away at that moment and so she had her opportunity to slip out of the room and escape from the old mansion. The day had been warm but the night was cold and had brought a heavy fog with it that cloaked the cove and the grounds.

As she hurried across the lawn she heard distant voices from down on the wharf. The crew were spending the first of many nights there aboard the tug and barge. Hearing them even from such a long way gave her some added courage. And she needed it. The grounds of Collinwood seemed more ghostly than usual on this eerie night.

She passed the stables and other outbuildings as she hurried on to the old house to warn Barnabas of what was going on. Along the way she began to worry that perhaps the gossip might be true, that there was a slim thread of fact in what they'd said. Barnabas might be a madman obsessed with the belief he was the original Barnabas Collins and a vampire. But that was preposterous! Barnabas was one of the most gentle men she'd ever met. She couldn't picture him harming anyone.

Yet he was supposed to be ill and he had been treated by Dr. Julia Hoffman. What nature had his illness taken? Had it been mental or physical, or both? Perhaps only Julia Hoffman knew for certain and it was doubtful if she'd reveal her knowledge to anyone else.

The grass was wet from the heavy fog and she could see barely a half-dozen feet in front of her. The foghorn at Collinsport Point was giving out its melancholy warning to add still another weird touch to the grim atmosphere of the night.

She was nearing the old house when she saw a sudden movement in the bushes on her left and halted. She waited, her heart pounding with terror, staring at the bushes and trying to tell herself there was no one there. But slowly the bushes parted to reveal the most macabre figure she had ever seen!

Norah cried out her fear at the sight of the dripping figure standing there only a short distance from her: a lovely, red-haired woman in the white flowing dress of a long-past era with an expression of hatred on her exquisitely-carved features. Strangest of all was the seaweed which clung to the long red hair and to her shoulders. The creature raised a hand to point at Norah!

And then she turned her head slowly so that Norah was able to see the other half of the lovely face. The revelation was sheer horror. No beauty lingered there. This side of the face was crushed and distorted and a bulging eye hung down on a sunken cheek!

"No!" Norah cried in protest.

There was no doubt in her mind that she was seeing the ghost of the female pirate, Jenny Swift! It had to be! The thing she saw answered all the descriptions she'd heard of the phantom creature. And now the ghost from under the sea began to drift slowly toward her.

Norah backed away. "Don't!" she begged the phantom.

But the weird apparition came relentlessly on toward her. With a scream Norah swung around and raced back in the direction from which she'd come. She was sobbing and running blindly through the fog-ridden grounds when she all at once stumbled into someone with an impact that nearly knocked them both over.

It was Captain Jim Donovan. Steadying himself and supporting her with a grasp on her arm, he stared at her with surprise.

"What's the matter, Miss Bliss?" he asked in amazement.

"Captain Donovan!" she cried in relief. Stifling her sobs as best she could, she glanced behind her. "I was threatened and then chased," she told him.

"By whom?"

She hesitated and then turned awkwardly and said, "I don't know exactly. It seemed like a ghost."

"A ghost?" The young man looked startled.

She was still afraid and yet somehow embarrassed. The phantom which had seemed so real only minutes ago, and which she could remember in shocking horror of detail, now struck her as unreal. The experience she'd just fled from had no solid basis in reality. She must have allowed her fears to make her see a ghostly figure where a moving bush had been. The fog played queer tricks with your vision.

Taking a deep breath, she said, "I've been foolish. You mustn't mind me. I allowed myself to be panicked by shadows."

Captain Donovan stared at her with concern. "You're certain it was nothing more than shadows?"

She was slowly regaining some poise. "Yes," she said. "I'm quite certain. I shouldn't have gone out walking alone on a night like this. I'm nervous in the dark."

"It is an unpleasant night," Donovan agreed. "I was on my way to the stables to see if they had any spare rope there. We need some and can't send for it until the morning."

She gave him a grateful look. "Again you came to my rescue in a time of crisis."

He smiled. "This wasn't much of a rescue."

"It was for me!" She shuddered, then forced a smile.

"I'd better walk you back to Collinwood," Captain Jim suggested.

She hesitated. "If you don't mind, I'd rather you escorted me as far as the old house. I want to speak to Mr. Barnabas Collins, who lives there."

"Sure. I don't think I've met him."

"Not likely. He's never around much during the days." I see."

She was pleased that he asked no questions about Barnabas. They talked of the salvage preparations as they gradually made their way back along the path on which she'd fled in terror. When they reached the point where she'd seen the phantom figure she became silent for a few seconds as she stared into the bushes. They were wreathed in fog and offered her no clue to what she'd seen there.

They approached the old house and she saw the tall, erect figure of Barnabas coming toward them. His gaunt face showed surprise at seeing her with the younger man.

When they met on the path, she said, "Good evening, Barnabas. You've warned me not to roam the grounds at night alone so I had Captain Jim Donovan bring me here. I don't think you two have met."

Barnabas stood there in his caped-coat studying them both

with his deep-set eyes. "No," he said. "We haven't met. But my servant, Willie Loomis, has mentioned you, Captain. We are all in your debt for your rescue of Norah this morning."

"That was nothing," the young man said.

"I heard the account differently," Barnabas assured him. "I think Norah should be much more careful when she's on that boat."

"I intend to be," she promised.

Barnabas gave her a bleak smile. "We know about your good intentions and how rarely you carry them out."

Captain Jim Donovan said, "I must be on my way, Miss Bliss." And to Barnabas, he added, "I've enjoyed meeting you, Mr. Collins."

"It has been a pleasure for me," Barnabas said in his resonant voice. "With your permission I'd like to visit the tug and inspect the diving bell. I hear it is of the latest design. Would it be too inconvenient if I came in the evening?"

"Not at all," the young Captain said. "At night we're always busy working on the equipment. It's a good time to take a look in it. Just ask for me and I'll show you around."

"Thank you," Barnabas said. "I'll remember that."

Jim Donovan said goodnight and went back along the path to vanish in the fog. Norah turned to Barnabas and said, "I know you warned me about coming out alone at night but I had to see you. Luckily the Captain came in time to escort me."

Barnabas gave her a searching look. "You're sure you didn't start here alone?"

She didn't want him to be angry with her, so she evaded a direct answer by saying, "I was glad when he came along."

"You look upset," Barnabas said, as they stood there in the heavy fog. "Is something wrong?"

"Yes. It's about what happened in the village last night."

"Oh?" His tone was restrained and his face was in shadow.

"You know what I'm talking about, don't you?" she asked anxiously.

"I think so." His voice was still taut.

"The girl who was attacked and a red mark left on her throat," she said. "Roger is blaming it on you. He says you've done things like that before, that you're mad and believe yourself to be the first Barnabas and a vampire." The man in the caped coat stood there in the shadows keeping his face concealed from her. In a dry tone, he commented, "It seems cousin Roger didn't leave much unsaid."

"Carolyn was angry. She told him he had no right to say such things."

"Carolyn is a fine girl."

"I couldn't get mixed up in an argument," she told him. "But I wanted to warn you. So I left the house as soon as I could. Roger is going to ask you to leave Collinwood."

"That's about what I'd expect," Barnabas said grimly.

She looked up at him with frightened eyes. "It's not true, is it?"

He looked resigned. "Do you want me to deny it?" "It's not really necessary," she said. "I know you're not well. But I can't believe you're mad."

"I'm not mad," he said quietly.

"I was sure of that," Norah said. "But I came here this afternoon and Dr. Julia Hoffman was here with you. I know I shouldn't have come, but I was jealous that you should give her privileges but denied me."

"She took the privilege. I didn't give it to her."

"She didn't explain that."

"Julia rarely explains anything." Barnabas hesitated. "What time were you here?"

"Late afternoon," she said. "I didn't get any further than the main cellar. Julia was in that room where she claims you sleep. She said you were ill and she'd been in to see if you'd improved. And she warned me that I mustn't disturb you."

"So?"

"I didn't," she said. "I left with her and I didn't see you at all."

"That was wise."

"But I've been worrying about you. Why don't you return to the clinic and see if Dr. Hoffman can help you? I know she wants to. She's in love with you, Barnabas." He allowed her to see his face and the sardonic smile on it. "You think so?"

"I know it."

"Perhaps," he said. "There are many urgent reasons why I can't enter the clinic at the moment. Maybe it will be possible later. I must try and find a way to get Roger to allow me to remain here. I don't want to leave until I learn what success you have with the treasure hunt." "

And I don't want you to leave," she said. "What will you do?"

Barnabas looked thoughtful. "I intend to check further on that David Cartill and his wife," he said.

Her face brightened. "You must! I think that is the way. Roger is already suspicious about the Cartills. If you could bring it out that David Cartill is really Quentin, then the attention would be taken from you for at least a little time."

"It's a possibility," Barnabas agreed. "I was on my way to the cottage area when I met you."

"That means we'll have no more time together tonight?" she said with some disappointment.

"I'm afraid so," Barnabas said. "But if I'm to get the solid proof against Quentin that I need I must give it some time."

"I understand," she said.

"So I'll see you back to Collinwood and then continue on to the cottage," he told her.

"You mustn't let yourself be seen at Collinwood," she worried. "Roger might come out and then you'd have the showdown you want to avoid."

"I'll take you close enough for safety," Barnabas said. "And I'll wait to see you go in."

"It's been a bad day," she said, her voice trembling as the vision of that terrifying ghost crossed her mind again. "Everyone is beginning to whisper about the curse."

"They're taking it more seriously?"

"Yes."

"I warned them," Barnabas said. "But they didn't want to listen. Not even your father."

She gave a tiny shudder. "There are times I wish he'd change his mind and decide to leave here. Then there'd be no more worries about phantoms."

"Your father refuses to believe in ghosts," Barnabas reminded her.

Her eyes were solemn. "I wonder if he'll feel the same way when he leaves here?"

"That's an interesting question."

When they reached Collinwood, he waited in the fog until she entered the house. She gave him a final wave at the door and he waved back. Then she went inside.

She found her father pacing up and down in the living room, waiting for her. He halted and glared at her as she entered. "Where have you been?"

"Out for some air."

"On this miserable night?"

"Yes. I had a headache."

Her father looked skeptical. "I was beginning to think you'd run off to the old house to see that Barnabas."

"I can't imagine why," she said.

"I know how you feel about him," her father informed her, "and I may say it worries me. I've been hoping you'd turn up shortly as we've had an invitation to go over and visit Carson Blythe and his foster daughter."

"Tonight?"

"Of course," her father said. "He phoned a short time ago and said he'd like to talk to us before we start tomorrow on the salvage work."

"Do you really want to go?" The idea didn't appeal to her.

"I think I should," Claude Bliss said. "And you ought to come along as well. We may pick up some interesting information. This fellow spent a lot of time trying to retrieve that treasure."

"He's so bitter about his failure," she protested. "He's twisted."

"I allow for that," her father said calmly. "He still could be of use."

She was in no mood to listen to the frail and broken Carson Blythe tell his ghost stories concerning the sunken Jenny Swift; she wanted to put ghosts and curses out of her mind until daylight, at least. But she disliked refusing this small cooperation with her father.

So she said, "Very well Let us go at once and get through with it as early as we can."

"We'll take the car," her father said. "It would be shorter to walk down the beach, but the tide is high and I don't know the way. So we'll take the long way around." It was nearly a fifteen-minute drive out to the road and then along to the side road leading to Blythe's mansion and in close to the cliffs again. The sprawling house of Carson Blythe was more modern than Collinwood, but no less imposing. It was built closer to the cliffs and had balconies and decks overlooking the ocean.

An elderly housekeeper admitted them and led them to a living room with a cathedral ceiling and great masses of glass in its walls. Carson Blythe was there to greet them with his foster daughter, Grace, standing beside him. The red-haired girl seemed pathetically glad to have company.

"I'm so glad you were able to come tonight," she said, as they were shown to chairs.

The white-haired Blythe was in his usual somber mood. "It had to be tonight if it were to do any good," he said, standing in the center of the room. "Even after your daughter nearly losing her life today, you're still determined to go on with the treasure hunt?"

"Definitely," her father said. "I can't allow an accident to frighten me into changing all my plans."

"There will be more accidents if you go on with it," Carson Blythe warned him.

"I'm not superstitious," her father said.

"I find that remark amusing," Carson Blythe said with sarcasm.

"Why?" her father asked.

"Because I have brought you here to show you the photograph of a ghost."

CHAPTER 8

Grace Blythe, who had been hovering nervously at the other side of the room, came over to her foster father and with a wan smile said, "I don't think you should excite yourself this way, Dad."

The white-haired man dismissed her with an annoyed glance. "I will not have you interfering in this," he informed her and then he turned to Norah's father again. "You wouldn't put me down as a crackpot, would you?"

Claude Bliss smiled. "Hardly."

"I can promise you that you shouldn't," the retired millionaire told him. "I have a reputation in the world of business. I'm still remembered as being one of the hard- headed ones."

"I can imagine," her father said.

Carson Blythe sank into a tall cane-backed chair of modem design and sighed. "I can tell you when I hit on the idea of recovering the gold and jewels from *The Jenny Swift* it was the blackest day of my life. My poor late wife tried to talk me out of the idea. But I wouldn't listen. I could picture myself making another easy fortune. Just as you are doing now, Mr. Bliss."

Her father looked embarrassed. "I don't think it is the money alone which interests me," he said. "The challenge has a meaning for me as well. Of course I do want the project to pay for itself and show a profit. But it doesn't have to do more. I'm running a salvage company twelve months of the year, year after year. I'm not a greedy fortune hunter, Mr. Blythe. I'm a businessman who happens to be in this line of venture."

The millionaire's thin face was grim as he listened. When her father had finished, he said, "And because you are in this as a business you think you'll have a better chance to succeed than those who have gone before you. You think you can lick the curse?"

"I suppose so."

Carson Blythe's lip curled with disdain. "Then you are a fool!"

"That's a harsh statement, Mr. Blythe," Norah commented mildly.

"I fully agree," Grace said, "and I think you should apologize."

Blythe looked embarrassed. "I'm sorry; a better word would have been foolhardy."

"I understand your strong feelings," Norah's father said. "And I sympathize with you."

"But you're still going ahead," Carson Blythe said.

"Yes."

The millionaire stared at him sadly. "You have the same attitude I had. You're just as impossible to reason with. Yet from the first day I sent a diving crew out to work on *The Jenny Swift* there were accidents. It began with the lines of one of the senior divers becoming fouled so that he nearly lost his life. That put him on the sidelines. After that a winch snapped and we lost a valuable trunk from the old vessel. I thought we were settling down to a regular routine when a bitter fight broke out between two of the crew. One went to the hospital with a knife wound and the other to jail."

Her father said, "But you wouldn't need a curse to make all these things happen. Every project has similar problems."

Carson Blythe smiled bitterly. "Sure, try to rationalize. That's what I did. But when it comes to a ghost it's extremely difficult to be rational. Especially when the mission of the phantom is to destroy your peace of mind and that of the people you love. Almost the moment we brought the first trunk up from the wreck my wife began to see the ghost of Jenny Swift."

"That had to be imagination," her father said.

The memory of her own awful experience so fresh in her mind, she turned to her parent and asked, "How can you say that when you know so little about it?"

Norah's father looked at her in bewilderment. "I have my firm beliefs."

Blythe smiled sourly. "And obviously they don't allow the existence of ghosts?"

"No." Her father was emphatic.

The white-haired millionaire squinted his eyes as he studied him. Then he said, "In a way I'm glad you did come here and that you're determined to carry on with the project. It will be almost worthwhile to see how quickly you'll be converted to a belief in the spirit world."

"I doubt that will happen," Claude Bliss said.

"I'm positive it will," Blythe said seriously. Turning to his foster daughter, he went on, "Grace will bear me out. From the moment my crew began the treasure hunt we were afraid to go on living here."

Norah was watching and listening closely. "It was that bad?"

"We were given no peace," he said dramatically.

Grace leaned on the back of her father's chair, her face doleful. "It's true. The ghost pursued us!"

Norah's father shook his head. "I'm sorry. Nothing but seeing the ghost for myself would convince me."

Carson Blythe stared at him with pity. "You will see that beautiful ruined face soon enough, believe me. And when she is not taunting you it will be your daughter who will suffer. She will torment her just as she did my wife."

Norah's father turned to her with a smile. "Have you any fear of this, my dear?"

Norah's face crimsoned. The horror of seeing what she believed was the ghost was still with her. "Mr. Blythe is making a strong case, but I suppose we will have to find out for ourselves."

"There you are," her father told the millionaire expansively. "My daughter isn't at all afraid."

She would have liked to have protested, "That's not true!" But instead she remained meekly silent.

"You're probably familiar with the mark of Jenny Swift's ghost," Carson Blythe said. "When she ruled that pirate ship she used a long black snake whip to keep the trash comprising her crew in line. And since she was killed in the wreck she's gone on using that whip for her vengeance on those who try to take her treasure."

"It's a colorful legend," Norah's father agreed.

The millionaire's expression was solemn. "I have seen dead men with the welt of that whip around their necks," he said. "And I saw one woman with it, my wife!"

"You blame your wife's death wholly on the ghost?" Norah asked.

"Yes."

"But she was a suicide!" Norah reminded him tactlessly.

"Hounded to her fate by Jenny Swift," Carson Blythe said brokenly. "Grace and I were seated down here when it happened. There was a scream from my wife's bedroom and a sharp sound like the snapping of a whip. Then my wife screamed again. We ran out on the deck and looked up at the balcony in time to see my wife plunge over to her death. But there was something in the shadows behind her!"

Grace had turned sickly pale. "Yes," she said in an awed whisper. "I saw it. It was the phantom."

"We both saw the ghost," the millionaire contended. "And as my wife went screaming to her death on the rocks below I heard a soft laugh from the shadows of the deck where that creature was standing. I swear it!"

"That's horrible," Bliss said after a moment. "But I think it all could be explained in a rational manner."

"You discount what Grace and I claim as eyewitnesses?" the millionaire said angrily.

"I'm sorry. I must." Her father looked uncomfortable. There was a long moment of strained silence in the high-ceilinged room. Carson Blythe hunched unhappily in his chair, his hands clutching the arms so tightly that his knuckles showed white. There was pain written on the fine-featured ascetic face.

Very slowly, he said, "My wife had a closed casket funeral, Mr. Bliss. Her face and body were too badly battered by the rocks to allow anything else. Restoration by the undertaker was hopeless. But when I went to her on the beach that night, I saw her. I steeled myself to examine the body before it was moved by the authorities and I swear a thick welt circled her throat! The welt of Jenny Swift's snake whip!"

Grace moved close and put an arm around his shoulders to comfort him. The pretty redhead said softly, "Don't! You mustn't think about it! Not ever again!"

"I'm sorry," Carson Blythe said brokenly and he bowed his head to hide his distress.

Norah's father got to his feet and she followed him. He said, "I'm sorry. Believe me I am. But I think this conversation is gaining us nothing. It is clearly upsetting to you and I can not change my plans because of it"

Grace said, "You must forgive him. Ever since it happened he has not been himself."

"No pity!" Carson Blythe said sharply and he stood up with an air of authority. "I've tried to warn you, Bliss. If you won't think of yourself, you should at least consider your daughter."

"My daughter is in agreement we should continue the treasure hunt."

Carson Blythe shook his head sadly. "You both have my sympathy."

"Thank you," Norah said. "We really should be going now. It's getting very late."

Grace came to escort them out "You must visit us again when I'm sure we'll have a more pleasant conversation."

Blythe turned his back on them and stood staring out at the fog-shrouded cove under whose waters the ancient vessel with its treasure lay. Grace, showing her embarrassment, saw them to the door and bid them a warm goodnight.

Neither of them spoke until they were in the car and headed back to Collinwood. Then Bliss said bitterly, "What a waste of time that was! I'd hoped to get some helpful technical information from him and all we heard was a lot of crazy ghost talk!"

She gave her father a frightened glance in the near darkness of the car's front seat. "Couldn't you tell that he is sincere in his warnings?"

"Sincere but slightly mad," Claude Bliss said with disgust. "His wife's suicide has left him unbalanced."

"I don't know," she said thoughtfully. "I feel there is something more." Again she wanted to tell him about her own frightening experience but didn't dare. "Still, I'm not sorry we made the visit."

"You're not?"

"Not really. It gave us a chance to know them better. The girl is surely attractive and very nice. I can't think what kind of life she can be having with him in this state. She should be away from that morbid atmosphere."

"He accuses me of being a thoughtless father, but he is more to be condemned."

"He probably doesn't realize how unfair he is being to her. And she is only a foster daughter. Yet sometimes adopted children can be more self-sacrificing than blood ones."

"Obviously in this case. Blythe is only a step or two from being a maniac."

They became silent again as they drove on through the fog to Collinwood. Norah worried that already they were beginning to have difficulty communicating. All her father could think of was the recovering of the treasure of the sunken pirate vessel, while she was caught between fear for what might happen to Barnabas Collins and what she might suffer from Jenny Swift's curse.

They arrived at Collinwood and left the car in the parking area. As they strolled to the front entrance of the mansion, her father said, "If it is wet and miserable tomorrow you'd better not plan to go out in the tug."

"But I always go along," she protested.

"After your accident I'm a little worried."

She gave him a quick glance. "Are you believing Carson Blythe in spite of what you said?"

"No," her parent said irritably. "I just don't enjoy the idea of you taking chances among cables and other equipment on wet, slippery decks."

"I'll manage very well," she promised him.

They went inside and the house was filled with midnight silence. Her father said goodnight to her on the murky landing and she went on to her bedroom. It had been a trying night and nothing really had been settled. In spite of herself she was gradually beginning to believe in the ghost—whose existence, she recalled, Barnabas had never denied.

Wondering how he had made out in his spying on David Cartill, she got ready for bed. The foghorn continued its melancholy blasts. Long after she had turned out the lights she tossed restlessly between the sheets. Then, finally, sleep came. But the kind of sleep that made her sigh and turn and murmur little frightened cries.

The phantom figure with the ruined face came to stalk her dreams—Jenny Swift, with the profile of beauty and the profile of a gargoyle at the turn of her head.

At last, morning came. And before she opened her eyes she could hear the rain. She raised herself up in bed with a frown and stared at the window. It was a torrential spring rain. Not an auspicious kind of day for beginning the salvage operation. Perhaps her father would decide to wait for another better day. She hoped so. But if he stubbornly insisted on beginning work, she wanted to take part.

She threw back the coverings, ready to get up and take a quick shower. And then she saw something that brought a look of fear to her lovely face. Strewn along the bottom of her bed were wet strands of seaweed. She couldn't believe her eyes. Getting up, she moved like a sleepwalker closer to the seaweed. She even reached out and touched its slippery reality.

Seaweed! Here in her room! She recalled her dreams and trembled at the thought that Jenny Swift had been here in the room. Then her eyes wandered across to an overturned chair. She had draped a dress on the back of it. Now the dress was on the floor ripped to shreds.

She looked around at the dresser and gasped as she realized its surface had been angrily swept clean of everything set out there. Her make-up, jewelry and other personal items were scattered on the rug by the dresser. She bent to recover her watch and saw that it had been deliberately smashed. The crystal was shattered and the face twisted to reveal the damaged inner mechanism. The destruction to her things had been thorough. And there on her bed was the calling card of her phantom visitor. Seaweed from the shoulders of Jenny Swift!

Norah was in a panic. What should she do? Who would she tell? It had to be a ghost! She'd locked the door. No one could have gotten into the room. But if she told her father he might not believe her. He might even think she'd arranged the destruction herself to stop him from going ahead with the project. Yet she had to talk to someone. Then she thought of Carolyn.

The maid, Lucy, would soon be arriving with the breakfast tray and if she got a glimpse of the destruction in the room there would have to be some explaining or she would spread all sorts of wild rumors. And this situation defied explaining. In desperation Norah slipped on a robe and went quickly to the door of Carolyn's room and knocked on it.

After a moment Carolyn opened the door, fully dressed. "Good morning. Isn't the weather dreadful?"

Norah nodded. "Yes. Can you come to my room with me for a moment? I have a problem."

Carolyn's eyebrows lifted. "Of course."

The maid had not yet appeared as Norah ushered the other girl into her room and after closing the door said dramatically, "What do you make of all this?"

Carolyn looked shocked as she gazed around her. "I don't get it!"

"Nor do I," Norah said. "I don't want Lucy to see it or she'll really do some talking."

"I know. This is crazy. Have you any idea who did it?"

"No. I slept through it all. Look at what is on the bedspread." She pointed to the seaweed.

"That's fantastic!" Carolyn gasped. "How did it get there?"

Norah gave her a meaningful look. "I haven't any idea, except it might have come on the shoulders of Jenny Swift. They claim her ghost is draped with wet seaweed."

"Oh, no!" Carolyn protested, fear shadowing her pretty face. "Perhaps Carson Blythe is telling the truth!"

There was a knock on the door. Norah said, "That will be Lucy." And she went and opened the door part way. "I'll take the tray here," she told the surprised girl. "I'm having a talk with Carolyn. You can come back for the tray later."

"Yes, miss," the stout girl said, staring in at Carolyn but not able to see the damage.

Norah shut the door and brought the tray into the room and sat it on its usual table. Then she turned to Carolyn. "At least that gets rid of her for a little."

Elizabeth's daughter was standing staring down at the seaweed with baffled eyes. "It's real!"

"Of course it's real!"

The girl looked at her with consternation. "It doesn't make sense. Are you sure you had your door locked?"

"Yes."

Carolyn made a despairing gesture at the seaweed. "Then this?"

"It had to come here by some supernatural means," Norah said calmly.

Wide-eyed, Carolyn protested, "But you are the one who said you didn't believe in ghosts."

"I think I do now," she said slowly, and then amended herself by adding, "I'm sure I do. I saw the ghost of Jenny Swift in the bushes near the old house last night"

"Truly?"

"Yes."

"Did you tell anyone?"

"No."

"Why not?"

She smiled forlornly. "They wouldn't have believed me. They won't even believe this. I had to talk to someone who might understand. I hoped you would. It's plain enough. Jenny Swift is angry at my father and she's striking at him through me, just as she attacked Carson Blythe by forcing his wife to suicide."

Carolyn stepped back from the bed. "It's all too creepy!"

"So the curse is real," Norah said. "Even the weather is terrible."

"What are you going to do?"

"Nothing, except clean up the mess. I wanted you to know in case something else should happen. Something I couldn't tell about."

Carolyn looked scared. "You mean if you are killed?"

"Or seem to have killed myself," Norah said. "You can't tell how it will go yet. At least I've had a warning. Next time she may not be content with that. She may decide to finish me."

The other girl moved across to her. "This is wild! You're talking as if you were dealing with a ghost!"

"I think I am."

"It has to be something different," Carolyn insisted. "Maybe the door wasn't locked as you thought. Someone got in. It has to be that."

Norah shook her head. "No."

"I'm still not convinced," the other girl said. "I want to help you."

"You can. Give me a hand in straightening up this mess," Norah said. She went and lifted the shreds of the once attractive dress. "I'll have to package this before I put it in the garbage, or it will cause awkward talk."

Carolyn was on her knees by the dresser. "It's just beyond belief."

After ten minutes of hard work they had removed most of the evidence of the midnight intruder's assault on the room. Then Carolyn went down to breakfast and left Norah to eat something from her tray.

It wasn't surprising that Norah found herself with little appetite. She drank her orange juice and coffee and then went downstairs. Her father was talking to Roger Collins, who seemed on his way out. As soon as Roger left, she went to her father.

"It's raining hard," she said. "Hadn't we better wait until tomorrow?"

Claude Bliss looked stubborn. "Why delay?"

She nodded towards the window where the rain was teeming down. "Isn't that good enough reason?"

"Not to halt underwater work," he said. "It makes no difference down there."

"You direct the operations from the tug," she reminded him.

"I'm not afraid of a little rain," he said. "And neither are the crew. We're going to begin on schedule."

She felt too depressed to argue. He would blunder straight on until disaster overtook the salvage attempt. "I'll meet you down at the wharf."

"I'd rather you didn't come today."

"If you're determined to work, I'm going along," was her answer. And she left him to go back upstairs and put on heavy slacks and her oilskin jacket and cap. It was the kind of day you had to be prepared for. There was nothing to do now but wait and see what happened.

As she finished getting ready the maid came back into the room to get the breakfast tray. Lucy picked it up and then gave her a strange look. "You hadn't much appetite this morning, miss."

She turned from the dresser mirror. "I wasn't hungry."

"You going out to the cove in this storm?" Lucy was surprised.

"Yes."

"It's a nasty day."

"I know," she said. "But they've decided to work."

Lucy lingered on. "I guess the fog and rain must have kept that monster from the village last night. There was no trouble like the night before."

"I'm glad of that," Norah said, wishing the girl would go.

"I say he'll come back," the stout girl insisted.

"Oh?"

"Yes. He did the same thing before. Skipped attacking anyone for a few nights and then came back. I say he'll do the same thing again. Those vampires are wily, miss." And with that bit of wisdom delivered, Lucy left with the tray.

Norah followed her downstairs but went straight outside. She flinched from the rain, even though she was dressed for it. Gingerly she made her way across the broad wet lawn to the edge of the cliffs. The steep path down the cliff face was made more dangerous by the rain. Its surface was slippery, yellow clay. Taking her time she managed to make her way to the beach without stumbling.

Smoke was pouring out of the tug's single funnel as it was readied to steam out to the spot in the cove where the treasure vessel had sunk. She was pleased to see that the rain had kept the curious away and there only the familiar crew members on the wharf.

Reaching the wharf, she met Captain Jim Donovan, who looked flatteringly pleased to see her. "Your father wasn't sure you'd be coming."

"He didn't want me to," she said.

"I'm glad you decided to join us," Jim said. "I'll help you aboard."

He gave her a steady hand to help her down onto the deck of the tug. She found it easier dressed as she was. But her father had been right; the tug's deck was as slippery as if it were covered with ice.

Her father was already on board supervising the way the diving bell would be towed. He gave her a troubled glance. "I see you've come."

"Yes."

He looked resigned. "Be careful."

"I will."

He went back to the men responsible for the bathysphere while it was being towed to position and she moved forward to stand in the bow of the large tug, feeling tense and upset. The teeming rain had at least dispersed the fog.

After a short time there were shouts from the dock and Captain Donovan jumped down to take over his role as skipper of the tug and assistant to her father in the salvage work. He came over to stand by her. "Well, we're getting under way," he said.

She nodded. "The suspense of beginning is over."

"And the real suspense starts." He called out some instructions to the crew and a moment later the tug pulled away from the wharf. The sturdy craft chugged across the choppy waters and the rain continued to come down.

It only took a few minutes for them to arrive at the buoy at anchor which had been set out to mark the position of the sunken Jenny Swift. The tug's engine was cut down as they began to get the diving bell into the proper place. One of the regular divers was standing by ready to go down and prepare the way for the diving bell.

Norah could remember when all the diving was done by these veterans. Her father came forward and gave some instructions to a member of the crew standing there. Then the diver was sent down for a preliminary survey in the area of the wreck.

Donovan took advantage of the lull to say to her, "We'll soon be sending the bathysphere down. Don't you wish you were going to be in it?"

She smiled. "It would depend on who I had for company. Are the telephones checked and working properly?"

"We've just made tests." The young captain smiled. "I wouldn't want any problems with them, since that is your department."

Norah didn't immediately answer him. Her attention had been taken by a line which had been pulled up from the water around the wreck. Clinging to it were strands of seaweed exactly like those she'd found on top of her bed!

CHAPTER 9

In spite of the rain, real progress was made that day in the salvage operation. The diving bell was sent down for a trial run and brought to the surface at the close of the afternoon. Norah sat in the single cabin of the tug, which her father used as an office, and took notes as one of the senior divers gave an account of what he'd discovered at the bottom of the cove.

The gray-haired diver's face wore a puzzled look as he said, "What surprises me is the amount of work that has been done down there."

Seated behind his small desk, her father said, "Explain that, Clary."

"Well, it's hard to pin right down. But I get the feeling this is ground gone over before. There's been a large opening cut in the side of the vessel and in the adjoining holds there's evidence of the contents having been removed. The ship seems pretty bare."

Her father frowned at this news. "You're suggesting that the other expeditions have already gotten what we're looking for?"

Clary nodded. "It could be."

"The records don't show it," Claude Bliss said. "The last salvage attempt was made by Carson Blythe. Up until then only a few gold coins and some fragments of jewelry had been recovered by earlier groups. Blythe's men came up with several trunks but they were disappointing as to contents. All they contained were iron chains, manacles and the like. Before he could proceed any further a storm came and destroyed so much of his equipment he gave up. At the same time he'd experienced grave personal tragedy."

"I heard about that," Clary said.

"So the treasure should be still somewhere in the holds of *the Jenny Swift*."

"Maybe," the diver said. "It's early in the game to say for sure. But I can tell the ship has been searched well. Could one of the earlier groups have found more than they admitted? That way they wouldn't have to answer to anyone for any share of the treasure."

Her father looked concerned. "I suppose that's possible."

"It has happened before," Clary pointed out.

Norah's father turned to her. "What do you think? That could be the reason Carson Blythe had such poor pickings. The treasure had been stripped from the vessel already."

She shrugged. "It is strange he didn't find more valuables. If only he were in a normal state of mind you could discuss this reasonably with him."

"I don't want to make the prospects seem black," the diver said. "But it's my job to tell you the truth. I don't think we're going to find much that is new down there."

Her father sat back in his chair with a sigh. "This is bad news."

"I could be wrong," Clary said unhappily.

"I realize that," Claude Bliss spoke thoughtfully. "But you have a great deal of experience. I don't like the report you've given me. Before we spend too much time and money on the project I'd like to have a talk with Blythe or whoever headed his salvage crew."

She said, "You should be able to discover who it was fairly easily."

"Yes," her father said. "We also should call in our backers and discuss this."

"Anything else, sir?" Clary asked.

"No," Bliss said. "Tomorrow I think I'll go down in the bathysphere. I want to take a look at the wreck again."

"Yes, sir," the diver said. And with a nod for Norah, he left the small cabin.

When he had gone her father spread his hands in a gesture of dismay. "What do you make of that?"

Her smile was bleak. "Bad luck seems to dog the project."

"I suppose we must expect that," Claude Bliss said. "The prophets of gloom would be disappointed if the curse didn't haunt us. As far as I'm concerned it's just plain bad luck."

"But you are going ahead?"

"Of course. One of the things I must do is try and get some

facts from Carson Blythe."

"Which means making an appointment with him."

"Something I don't look forward to," her father said. "I'll go alone this time and maybe I'll be able to communicate with him more successfully."

"I hope so," she said. "But I wouldn't count on it."

Her father got to his feet with a bitter smile. "It seems we'd be wise not to count on anything."

They returned to the house on the cliffs. Roger Collins was waiting to greet them and hear the reports of the day's progress. When her father told him what had gone on, Roger stared at them with some dismay. "Then all this effort may have been for nothing?"

"That's entirely possible," her father agreed.

"Annoying," the stern-faced Roger said. "I'd better phone Dr. Hoffman and Professor Stokes and have them come here for a council of war. They should be frankly told of the development."

"I thoroughly agree," her father said.

"Neither the doctor nor the professor are poor people," Roger said with some concern. "Still, I'd dislike seeing them pour more of their capital into something which has no chance of showing a return."

Norah, still in her working clothes of oilskins and slacks, said, "There is always a large amount of speculation with treasure hunts. The gamble is great."

"True," Roger Collins said. And then he told her father, "There was a long distance call from New York for you. A number was left for you to get in touch with." "Probably my lawyer with a report on the Cartill business,"

Bliss said. "I'll take care of the call." And he left them.

When they were alone, Roger remarked, "You look very much at home in that sailor's outfit, Miss Bliss."

"I wear things of this type regularly on the tug."

"A strange occupation for a woman."

"I enjoy it. It has a real fascination."

Roger Collins frowned. "Indeed it has. I find myself attracted to the treasure hunt in spite of Carson Blythe's woeful predictions. But I hope it doesn't turn out to have more glamor than treasure."

"You can never be sure," she said. "Did you manage to see Barnabas Collins last night?"

"No," he said, still looking concerned. "I went to the old house and tried to talk to him but he'd gone out somewhere. He can be hard to locate when he likes."

"Was everything quiet in the village?" She knew that it had been from the maid's report but wanted to hear his comment anyway.

"It was quiet," he admitted reluctantly. "But the trouble could resume again at any time. I'm still going to search Barnabas out and have a serious talk with him."

At that moment his son, David, came in to join them. Smiling bashfully at her, he said, "You're dressed like a man."

She laughed. "I am at that. I must hurry upstairs and change or I'll be late for dinner."

David, standing beside his father, wanted to know, "Can I go out on the tug one day?"

"If your father gives you permission," she said. "It can be dangerous out there."

Roger put a hand on the boy's shoulder. "We'll think about that later," he said. "There'll be lots of time."

"Of course," she said with a final smile for them before going upstairs.

It was pleasant to take a warm shower and change into a chic wool dress for dinner. It had been wet and miserable on the tug, and there was still a drizzle in the air with the fog partially returned.

She wondered what her father would say if she were frank with him about her experience with the ghost of Jenny Swift. He'd probably find some way to prove she was allowing her imagination to run away with her, she concluded.

A soft knock came on her door. When she called "Come in," Carolyn slipped into the room closing the door almost furtively behind her.

"Anything new?" she asked.

"Not a thing."

Carolyn's pretty face showed her uneasiness. "I've been thinking of what happened here all day. I can't get it out of my mind."

"I didn't mean to worry you," Norah said.

"Who could have done it?"

"I'd rather not try to guess that just yet."

"Aren't you afraid to sleep here again tonight?" Carolyn wanted to know.

She smiled ruefully. "I can't say that I'll look forward to it. But I must. It's one way of finding out what it means and if there'll be any more such visitations."

"The ghosts of Collinwood," Carolyn said with a tiny shudder. "You know, the villagers have always claimed this house is haunted."

"Most old houses have the same reputation," Norah said. "I don't think we should dwell too much on it until we learn more about the haunting."

They went down to dinner. At the table the talk was mostly about the weather and the happenings at the fishpacking plant. Roger Collins did mention that Dr. Hoffman and Professor Stokes were driving over for a meeting later in the evening. Norah was thinking about Barnabas and wondering whether she'd have the opportunity of seeing him. She badly wanted to discuss the things that had happened with him.

Almost as soon as they finished with dinner, Dr. Julia Hoffman and Professor Stokes arrived. They gathered in the living room for a general discussion. Her father spoke first.

He said, "There is one thing I should let you all know at once. My lawyer called me and he informs me there is a David Cartill resident in Barbados. And he does have a wife, Belle, who is descended from an ancient Barbados family."

Roger Collins looked worried. "Then this fellow's claim may be sound?"

"I don't know," her father replied. "According to my lawyer, the couple are away from the island on holiday and so he wasn't able to contact them personally."

Professor Stokes said, "Then that confirms what we know. Cartill and his wife are living here."

Bliss said, "The Cartill here and his wife could still be impostors. No one seems able to say where the Cartills are visiting. They could be in Europe."

"Then we really don't know anything more than before," Elizabeth said with a troubled note in her voice.

Julia Hoffman joined in the conversation. "We know there are such people and Cartill's claim to part of the treasure in his wife's name may be a genuine one."

Roger Collins looked grim. "Which brings us to the point of my calling this meeting. Will there actually be any treasure?"

"What do you mean?" Astonishment was written all over Professor Stokes' florid face.

"Yes." Julia leaned forward in her chair. "That statement calls for explaining."

Roger glanced at Norah's father. "I think you should take over."

Claude Bliss nodded and sighed heavily. "To be completely honest, the findings of my chief diver have been disappointing so far. He thinks *The Jenny Swift* was stripped bare of treasure by someone who was here before us."

Professor Stokes blustered, "But there are no records of any treasure being found."

Dr. Julia Hoffman gave him a smiling rebuke. "Professor Stokes, you mustn't be so naive! What Mr. Bliss is trying to tell us is that someone may have found the treasure and succeeded in keeping it a secret."

The professor's mouth gaped open. "Carson Blythe?"

Norah's father shook his head. "No. I'd eliminate Blythe. It had to be someone who worked on the wreck before him. Over the years there have been at least six or seven salvage attempts."

"I'm sure we all agree it is grim news," Roger Collins said.

Julia Hoffman turned to Norah's father. "What do you think?"

"I'm worried," he said.

"Is there any chance of treasure at all?"

"There could be. I've enough faith to go on with our exploration of the wreck."

"In that case," Julia Hoffman said, "I'm willing to continue my financial support of the salvage. What about you, Roger?"

"I'll continue," Roger said.

"And you, Professor?" the doctor asked her associate.

Professor Stokes considered for a moment. "Very well. I assume if you find any more evidence to support the theory the vessel is empty of treasure you'll cut short the operation. And that will mean less financial outlay for us?"

"I guarantee that," Norah's father said. "But that's all I can guarantee. I plan to talk to Carson Blythe and the man who headed his salvage team. I may get valuable information from them."

"Then we can leave it at that," Roger Collins said.

They broke up into smaller groups then, and Norah found herself in a shadowed corner of the big living room with Dr. Julia Hoffman.

The doctor asked, "Have you seen Barnabas?"

"Very briefly."

"How did he seem?"

"A little upset. I'm sure he's worried about the rumors in the village."

"Naturally," Julia Hoffman said.

"And he's very suspicious of David Cartill," Norah said. "He believes him to be Quentin Collins."

Julia hesitated over the thought. Then she said, "Why not? Quentin enjoys nothing more than upsetting Roger. This could be another of his pranks."

Norah said, "As for myself, I'm beginning to have a healthy respect for the ghost of Jenny Swift."

"You believe her curse is on us all?"

"I'm wondering."

"Then you must have seen or heard something?" the doctor suggested.

"Perhaps."

Before the woman doctor could put any further questions to her the housekeeper came into the living room and announced, "Mr. Cartill to see Mrs. Stoddard or Mr. Collins."

Roger was nearest to the double doors leading from the entrance hall. He said, "You may show Mr. Cartill in." The housekeeper vanished and a moment later David Cartill strode into the room, looking angry. He glanced from Roger Collins to the rest of them.

He said, "I asked to speak to you alone."

Roger said, "These are my friends. They are all interested in the treasure hunt. So you may speak plainly before them."

The good-looking young man hesitated, then said, "You're sure you wish me to speak frankly here?"

"Please do," Elizabeth Stoddard said, moving to a position beside her brother. "These are all our friends and associates. We have no secrets from them."

"I congratulate you, madam," David Cartill said with irony. "Few people would dare be in your position."

"Let's stop bandying words," Roger Collins said crossly. "Why have you come here?"

"I warned you I would be an interested spectator of the salvage, and that I would be open to any reasonable offer to settle my wife's claim to the treasure."

"If she has such a claim, Mr. Cartill," Dr. Hoffman said sharply.

"She has, no question of it," David Cartill told her. "But I no longer feel as friendly to your group as I did the other day."

"Really?" Elizabeth said. "Why not?"

"Because of a grave injury done to my wife," Cartill said angrily.

His answer was so completely unexpected that it caused a moment of concerned silence in the big room. Norah could tell by the expression on her father's face and the looks of the others that they were all as baffled as she by his angry words.

It was Roger who spoke up first. "What injury has been done to your wife?"

Cartill looked at him grimly. "Last night, while I was away from the cottage for a brief time, my wife was attacked and left semiconscious in our kitchen. And she had a strange red mark on her throat."

"Why blame us?" Roger demanded.

The young man smiled in a threatening fashion. "Because I'm not so new to the area as not to have heard about your mad cousin Barnabas, Mr. Collins. I know what he has done before and what he is doing now. I will not have him robbing my wife of her life's blood to satisfy his nightmarish needs!"

Norah felt she might faint. It was too awful to hear Barnabas spoken of in this manner. And yet the young man's rage seemed honest—and, if what he said was true, then surely justified. But how could she know? His wife, Belle, had been a creature of mystery from the start.

Norah's father broke the stunned silence which had again come to the room. He said calmly, "I'm afraid you've been listening too much to the village gossip. There is no evidence to connect Barnabas Collins with these attacks."

"I wonder," David Cartill said nastily. "The police seem to think so."

"The police question many people in incidents of this sort," Roger Collins said at once. "That by no means indicates they are guilty or have even been associated with the crime."

"I knew you'd deny everything," David Cartill said. "And you are fortunate that my wife has come out of the attack with no lasting effects. But I warn you, it has changed my entire attitude."

Norah's father said, "In what way?"

"I'll not be satisfied with a small share of the recovered treasure," David Cartill told him. "I'll want the major part of it."

"You're presuming a good deal," Professor Stokes blurted angrily.

David Cartill gave him a cold smile. "I merely wanted to advise you all of the change in the situation."

Roger Collins intervened, "I'd like to advise you of a change you are surely not aware of. The findings of the divers have not been satisfactory. The plain fact of the matter, Mr. Cartill, is that there may be no treasure to quarrel over."

The young man showed no distress at the news, only scorn. "I had an idea you'd try some tricks."

"This is no trick," her father hastened to assure him. "Mr. Collins has given you the facts. So all your threats may be for nothing."

"I can bide my time, Mr. Bliss," Cartill said calmly. "I haven't a doubt the treasure is still buried deep in the hold of *The Jenny Swift*. When you bring it to the surface I'll be there to claim what is rightfully ours. Good evening to you all." He bowed and left the room.

When the front door slammed after him there was a general murmuring among them. Roger Collins turned to her father and said, "This is a nice development, I must say. I only wish we knew whether that young man is genuine or a swindler!"

"My lawyers will find out," her father said.

"In the meanwhile it is most uncomfortable for us all," Elizabeth Stoddard said.

Roger seemed in a rage. "Depend on Barnabas to do something this stupid!"

"Cartill may be lying about his wife being attacked," Julia Hoffman reminded him.

Norah felt a surge of hope. She exclaimed, "I think so, too. He heard the village talk about the other night and decided to capitalize on it."

Carolyn came to her support. "Of course, Uncle Roger. He's made it up as an excuse to demand more of the treasure."

Professor Stokes turned to Roger. "What do you think?"

Roger Collins shook his head worriedly. "I don't know. He could have done that. On the other hand we know that Barnabas has this horrible weakness. There was the girl attacked in the village. Why couldn't he have gone to the cottage and made Mrs. Cartill his victim last night?"

"It's a dreadful predicament," Elizabeth mourned.

Julia gave Norah a meaningful glance and they both slowly made their way out of the living room. When they were in the privacy of the entrance hall the doctor whispered, "I mean to find Barnabas and question him. Do you wish to come along?"

"Yes," Norah said.

Julia Hoffman eyed her sadly. "I know you're my rival for his affections, but we can forget that for the moment. Because we both love him we should join in our efforts to help him."

"I agree."

"It's still drizzling a little," the woman doctor said. "You'll need your raincoat. Get it and I'll meet you just outside."

"I won't be a minute," she promised.

The others were still in the living room talking when she tiptoed down the stairs and went out to join the woman doctor. Julia was a few steps from the door and came out of the shadows as soon as Norah appeared. Together they set out for the old house.

As they walked through the drizzle and fog, Norah said, "I'm sure we'll find out David Cartill is an impostor."

"I agree," Dr. Hoffman said. "He is much too good to be true. He plays the role like an actor."

"Barnabas says it's Quentin."

"I'm inclined to think so."

"Yet there are Cartills. Father's lawyer has confirmed that much."

"I know," Julia replied. "The problem will be to protect Barnabas until we really discover the truth."

There was a certain eeriness about the foggy night that made Norah nervous. Her meeting with the phantom along this same isolated path kept coming back to her. She could picture that beautiful ghostly face with its mutilation so horribly revealed at a twist of the phantom's head. Collinwood was surely a place of ghosts!

They reached the entrance to the old red brick house and Julia mounted the steps and rapped on the door. After a moment there was the sound of shuffling footsteps and the door was opened. Willie Loomis glanced out from a narrow slit of the doorway.

"Yes?" he asked in his nervous fashion.

"Where is Barnabas?"

"Not here."

"Where has he gone?" Julia Hoffman asked.

"He didn't say," Willie replied sullenly.

"You always know." Julia's tone was firm.

The youth in the doorway hesitated. "Maybe he went to the old cemetery."

"Are you sure?" Julia asked.

"Yes," Willie said and he shut the door in their faces.

Julia turned to Norah with a bleak look. "It took long enough to find that out. His manners are not the best. I can't imagine why Barnabas tolerates him."

"He says he is trustworthy," Norah said.

"He must have some virtue," the older woman agreed. She stared out into the fog. "Are you willing to go to the cemetery?"

"If Barnabas is there."

"I warn you, it isn't a pleasant place and it's a long way from this house and even further from Collinwood. You could scream forever and it's very unlikely anyone would hear it."

"We have each other for company," she said, though she was feeling more nervous every minute.

"I know," Julia Hoffman said. "We should be all right. I only hope that Willie told us the truth and Barnabas is there."

They left the steps of the old red brick house and began crossing the field that slanted down towards the cemetery. Norah had heard of the ancient graveyard but had never visited it.

Julia marched a step ahead of her. "The gates of the cemetery are only a few feet away," she said.

"Why should Barnabas want to come here on a night like this?" she asked the other woman.

Dr. Hoffman was slow in replying. Then she said, "It is something in his nature. He is a person who dwells much in the past. Memories affect him a great deal."

"They must, to bring him here in the darkness," she worried. Julia Hoffman gave her a sympathetic glance. "You must try to understand. Here are the cemetery gates." Norah hesitated for a brief moment as she saw the stone columns and the iron gates ajar. Beyond loomed the ghostly tombstones. A tightness gathered at her throat. And she had the feeling that within those gates not Barnabas but the phantom figure of Jenny Swift awaited her.

CHAPTER 10

D r. Julia Hoffman turned to glance at her again. "Are you so terribly afraid of cemeteries?" she asked.

Norah shook her head. "No. I'll be all right." But that terrible fear still haunted her.

Julia continued to lead the way. The ground was wet and the tombstones glistened with dampness. She moved amid the forest of granite slowly, peering through the heavy mist to catch some sign of Barnabas.

"I have no idea where he might be here," she said.

Norah glanced around apprehensively. "Perhaps he didn't come here at all. Willie may have been wrong."

"Or deliberately misled us," Julia said bitterly.

They passed the solemn white figure of a granite angel whose lifelike face seemed to stare at them from a blanket of fog. More and more Norah felt that they should never have come to the graveyard at this late hour. She thought she heard a movement on her right and quickly turned to gaze in that direction. But there was nothing but the melancholy vista of leaning headstones.

Then she glanced back to check with Julia Hoffman, but the doctor was nowhere in sight. She had vanished! Fear clutched at Norah's heart and she stood there searching the foggy darkness for some sign of her friend.

"Julia!" she called. Then, "Dr. Hoffman!" But there was no reply.

Fear crept across her pretty face. This was unbelievable! Hysteria clamored to take Norah over. "Where are you?" she cried. And only the echo of her own voice came to her mockingly.

She didn't know what to do. Almost too frightened to move, she stood there waiting. But there was no sound, no clue to suggest where the woman doctor might have gone. Had Julia deliberately deserted her out of jealousy of her and Barnabas?

It was a terrifying thought and probably not fair to the woman doctor. Without warning a night bird flew above the cemetery, coming close to her head with a frenzied screeching. Norah crouched frantically to escape it; the spell broken she began to run sobbing along one of the winding cemetery paths.

"Dr. Hoffman!" she screamed out again.

She'd known it was useless, but it had at least helped as a release of her taut fear. Now she stumbled and fell outstretched before a broken headstone. She lay there sobbing for a moment or two before she was able to drag herself up from the wet ground and move on.

Soon she was in the area of the tombs. They loomed out of the dark and mist in haunting fashion. She was about to turn and try to find her way out of the cemetery when she saw a terrifying figure coming toward her from behind the shelter of one of the tombs.

It at first seemed like a man and then she saw the face. It was that of a wild animal, hairy and with animal features. A face that was a cross between a human and some denizen of the forest. Great hairy hands reached out to grasp her. At the sight of the forbidding monstrous claws she began screaming again and backing away. A snarling chuckle came from the thing's twisted mouth as it advanced toward her.

She continued to retreat, but the thing came nearer with every step and she knew she could not escape it for much longer. She fell back against a gravestone and the monster snarled again and bore down on her!

Norah cried out her terror and fought back as she was gathered up in its arms. The thing lifted her as if she weighed nothing and while she continued to struggle it began moving deeper into the cemetery. Norah was sure this was going to mean her death. She was experiencing the full fury of the pirate curse!

"Norah!" She heard her name called from a distance in the familiar voice of Barnabas.

"Barnabas!" she screamed back before a hairy hand was clamped over her mouth. Then she blacked out.

When she opened her eyes again, Barnabas had her cradled in his arms as he bent over her on the ground. She stared at him dully for a moment.

Then she murmured, "The monster!"

"He's gone," Barnabas said. "As soon as he heard my voice he dropped you. By the time I reached you he had run for cover."

Fear distorted her lovely face. "It was horrible! A face like an animal!"

"I know," he consoled her. "It will be all right. What attacked you was Quentin in the werewolf state which occasionally overcomes him."

"Quentin!" she gasped.

"Yes. He must have followed you here. When he is in that state he's not responsible for his actions."

Memory returning, she was freshly alarmed, "Julia Hoffman! She was with me and she vanished!"

Barnabas showed concern. "You're sure?"

"Yes. All at once I couldn't find her!"

He glanced around in the foggy darkness. "She must be here somewhere."

"Where?"

"Will you be all right if I look around for a few minutes?" Barnabas asked.

"Yes," she said weakly. "Be careful!"

He nodded. "I'll be all right." And his tall figure vanished in the fog.

Feeling ill and exhausted, Norah got to her feet. If she'd been attacked by Quentin in his werewolf state, she reasoned dully, then certainly Quentin had to be at Collinwood. It meant that he really was posing as David Cartill. Surely her father and the others would believe that now.

Trembling, she waited for Barnabas to come back. The minutes seemed to drag by. Then when she felt her nerves wouldn't stand it any longer Barnabas emerged from the darkness and fog carrying Julia Hoffman in his arms. Norah rushed over to him. "Is she seriously hurt?"

Barnabas glanced grimly at his burden. "She's had a bad blow on the head. I found her unconscious hidden by a gravestone. No doubt Quentin tackled her before he came after you."

"But why?"

"When he has these spells he's insane," Barnabas told her. "The best thing I can do is get Julia back to Collinwood as quickly as possible. Professor Stokes is there, isn't he?"

"Yes."

"He'll know how to treat her," Barnabas said. "We can only hope the damage isn't severe."

"Can you carry her back all that way?" Norah worried.

"I'll manage," he said. "Let's get started."

They left the cemetery and made their way up the steep field. When Barnabas reached the old house, he rested for a few minutes, depositing Julia on its front steps.

Turning to Norah he asked, "Why were you two in the cemetery?"

"Looking for you."

"For me?" He sounded surprised.

"Yes. Willie said you were there."

"Why did you want to see me?"

"Because David Cartill came to Collinwood and denounced you as the attacker of his wife. He made a very convincing scene of it."

Barnabas looked grim. "Quentin again."

"Will the others believe that? There has been no evidence yet to disprove Cartill's claim to the treasure."

"So he still has the advantage over us," Barnabas said.

"I'm afraid so," she admitted. "Perhaps it would be better to say we have no idea who attacked us in the cemetery. I doubt if Julia did see him before he rendered her unconscious. That way we'll get sympathy without arguments!"

Barnabas said, "You have a realistic outlook." And he picked up the still-unconscious Julia. "I should be able to make it all the way this time."

And he did. They reached the entrance of Collinwood about ten minutes later. Barnabas carried Julia inside. The moment Professor Stokes saw her he was all professional.

Elizabeth found her a bedroom and had her installed in it. A maid brought up hot water and the other things the Professor requested for his medical examination of the injured woman. The rest of them waited downstairs. At last the professor returned to join them.

"She's had a minor concussion," he said. "But she's conscious again and she'll be all right."

"Thank Heaven for that!" Roger Collins said.

"I have given her a sedative," Professor Stokes told them. "She should sleep until morning. By then she ought to be her normal self."

Barnabas had stood by quietly waiting for the news. He said to Stokes, "Thanks. Just so I know she's out of danger. Now I'll be on my way."

Before he could leave, Roger Collins came across the room to him. "You're not expecting to get off that easily, are you?"

Barnabas stared at him. "What do you want, Roger?"

"Who attacked those women tonight?"

Norah answered, "We couldn't see."

Roger eyed her sternly. "I was questioning Barnabas."

"He doesn't know!" she protested.

Roger said, "He's supposed to have been your rescuer."

"He did rescue us!"

"Then he must have some idea what or who attacked you," Roger insisted stubbornly. "What have you to say to that, Barnabas?"

Barnabas had a worn look on his handsome face. "I suggest you watch David Cartill more closely."

Roger gave a nasty laugh. "And he was here not long ago suggesting the same thing about you. He claimed you'd attacked his wife."

"I did not."

"You wouldn't be fool enough to admit it if you were guilty," Roger growled. "I know there are things going on here which shouldn't be. And I blame you for part of it."

Barnabas shrugged. "If you find it convenient."

"I think it's true," Roger snapped.

"There's nothing for me to say," Barnabas told him, "beyond goodnight." And with that he turned and started out. Roger crossed to Norah's father in exasperation while on sudden impulse Norah decided to follow Barnabas out. She didn't care what the others thought or said!

Barnabas had gone quite a distance across the lawns toward the cliff before she reached him. She was panting from her exertions when she caught up to him.

"I had to catch you," she said.

He halted and gave her a reproving look. "You shouldn't have come out here."

"I wanted to talk to you."

"What will they think?"

"I don't care!"

"You should."

"They know how I feel about you. That I'm on your side," she insisted. "Perhaps even that I'm in love with you!"

He gave a deep sigh and resumed walking toward the cliff path with her at his side. He said, "What happened tonight should convince you that this place is truly under a curse. You should persuade your father to take you away from here."

"Father won't leave until he winds up the search for the treasure."

"Then it may be too late."

"Barnabas!" She pulled at his arm plaintively.

He halted again. "Yes?"

"Won't you stand still a moment so I can talk to you?" she pleaded.

He stood there in the fog, a darker shadow outlined against the dim hulk of Collinwood with its orange squares of window lights. He said, "What I should do is take you straight back to your father."

"There are things I must tell you," she insisted. "I saw the ghost the other night. And last night she came to my room and destroyed a lot of things and left seaweed on my bed."

"You saw the ghost of Jenny Swift?"

"Yes!" And she proceeded to tell him about it in detail as they stood there on the edge of the cliffs.

"This is very bad," Barnabas said, when she'd finished.

"There will be more deaths unless your father is persuaded to give up the treasure hunt."

"You felt it was a good idea in the beginning?" she reminded him.

"I didn't understand things as well as I do now," Barnabas said. "And according to what your father says there seems little hope of much treasure being found in any case."

"He wants to be sure."

The foghorn on Collinsport Point came in with a mournful blast. And from down on the wharf a few of the colored lights on the tug could be faintly seen through the mist. The distant sound of a radio playing country music reached them.

Barnabas said, "Everything points to danger. Yet there's nothing I can do to prevent it if your father refuses to leave."

"He will refuse."

His handsome face was solemn. "Then you must be more careful than ever. Going to the cemetery, even with Julia as company, wasn't very smart."

"We both wanted to see you."

"I would have come around to Collinwood in due time or at least sent Willie with a message. You mustn't be so impatient."

"I'll remember," she promised.

"If I was sure I could depend on that," Barnabas said. "The first thing I want to do is prove Quentin is David Cartill. After that I'll try to solve the mystery of Jenny Swift's ghost."

"Why do you place so much importance on exposing Quentin?" she asked.

"Because he is complicating things here for his own amusement," Barnabas said. "And this is not a humorous predicament we're finding ourselves in."

"If he isn't really dangerous, does it matter?"

"Look what he did to Julia tonight," Barnabas reminded her. "And you would have suffered more if I hadn't come to your rescue."

Her face shadowed. "I can't believe that mad creature was Quentin!"

"He probably won't believe it either, when he comes out of his spell," Barnabas said bitterly. "That's another reason why he's pure menace."

"I suppose you know best."

"And now I want you to go back to Collinwood," he said.

"I'd rather remain here with you."

"And I'd like to have you, but it isn't practical," he said. "I'll walk you back part way."

Norah looked up at him with a pleading smile. "Father won't take me away from here, Barnabas. Why don't you do it?"

"I'd like to. Believe me."

"I'll go with you anywhere. We can be married and have a wonderful life."

"It's not that simple," he said, his face sad. "Come along. I'll go some of the distance with you."

She didn't move, her eyes fixed on his. "Kiss me, Barnabas," she murmured.

"You're being very unfair, my darling," he said heavily. But he did take her in his arms for a lasting embrace and his kiss was ardent enough. At last he released her and abruptly began leading her back to Collinwood.

When they were within a few yards of the front door he halted. She turned to him. "How long before I see you again?"

"Soon."

"That's really no answer," she protested.

"I'll be in touch with you all the time," he said. "I promise."

"I'll count on you," she said.

"Talk to your father," he reminded her. "Try to get him to leave."

She sighed. "I'll try."

He touched his lips briefly to hers again and then she hurried to the front door of the old mansion and went inside. There she found Professor Stokes waiting for her.

The professor said, "I've been hoping you'd return soon. You caused quite a situation when you rushed out after Barnabas."

"I had to talk to him alone," she said with some defiance.

Professor Stokes looked surprised. "I see," he said. "Julia has been asking to speak to you. I think you'd better stop by her room even though it's late. She will be returning to the clinic with me first thing in the morning."

Norah raised her eyebrows. "Is she well enough to travel?"

"The short journey won't hurt her," he said. "She's coming around very quickly."

"I'd still think it would be a risk."

"Not really," the professor said. "You will stop by and see her? You know the room?"

"Yes. It's the guest room at the head of the stairs on the third floor," Norah said. "I'll go up there now."

The door of the bedroom was slightly ajar and she went directly into the softly lighted room. Julia Hoffman's head was propped up on a pillow and she had a damp cloth resting on her forehead. Seeing Norah enter, she took the cloth off and raised herself on an elbow.

"I told the professor to have you come here," she said.

Norah was concerned. "You shouldn't sit up like that."

"I'll be all right," the woman doctor said. "Did you see who it was who attacked us in the cemetery?"

"Yes. I told the others I didn't."

Julia nodded wisely. "I guessed it had to be something like that. Why?"

"Barnabas felt they wouldn't believe me."

"Barnabas probably was right," the woman doctor said. "Go on. Tell me about it."

"There was a kind of monster, with the body of a man and the face of an animal, in the cemetery. Barnabas claims it was Quentin under the werewolf curse."

"I've heard something of that."

"It doesn't seem possible," she said, still bewildered.

"Many of the things which happen here seem impossible," Julia warned her. "But they continue to happen."

"Professor Stokes says you're returning home in the morning."

"Yes. I'm well enough to travel. It wasn't a bad bump, even though I was unconscious much too long." She gave her a bleak smile. "And you'll have Barnabas to yourself again for a while."

"I hardly see him."

"I know," Julia Hoffman agreed. "You must be very careful. Especially with Quentin still here. You never can be sure about him."

"So it seems," Norah sighed. Then she said goodnight and went on to her own room.

She took every precaution, locked the door and all the windows, and even left a light burning in the bathroom. She finally slept and her sleep carried on through until Lucy arrived with her tray the next morning. It had been a completely quiet night for a change.

As Lucy prepared her tray the maid said, "Professor Stokes and Dr. Hoffman left a few minutes ago."

She was surprised. "I didn't think they'd go this early."

"Professor Stokes had some urgent early appointments at the hospital."

"I see," she said, sitting down to the tray.

Lucy regarded her with interest. "You were in the cemetery when she was attacked, weren't you?"

"Yes," she said, hoping the maid wouldn't press her with questions.

"Did you see who did it?"

"Not really. I just missed her."

"Oh!" Lucy seemed disappointed. "A lot of us downstairs thought it was Barnabas who must have attacked her."

"You were very wrong in that," she said indignantly. "It was Barnabas who came to our rescue."

"I'm sorry, miss," Lucy apologized. "I didn't know."

"People who don't know shouldn't be so ready to gossip," Norah said with a hint of acid in her tone.

Lucy looked abject. "I'm sorry, miss," she repeated as she hurried out.

Norah watched after her grimly. It was this kind of loose gossip which had caused Barnabas so much trouble. Undoubtedly he'd been linked with crimes many times when he was completely innocent. At least this once she'd been able to defend him.

It was a fine day and everyone arrived at the wharf early. Captain Donovan was there to supervise the preparations for the day and he wasn't too busy to greet her with a smile.

"Looks as if our luck has changed," he said.

She returned his smile. "On the surface, at least. Let's hope we locate something of interest in the wreck."

"I hope so," he said. "We're sending a full crew down this morning. We ought to know more by the end of the day."

Norah was aboard the tug when it moved out into the cove to the spot where centuries ago the pirate vessel had foundered. When they reached the marking buoy her father began arranging for the diving bell and the divers to be sent down. He was also making the descent with them.

Norah stood by him, somewhat worried. "Do you need to go down there?"

"Yes," he said. "I want to get a better idea of the wreck and the condition it's in. This is a sunny day and the water at the bottom shouldn't be as hard to see in as before. Even with our floodlights it was difficult when it was raining."

"What will you do if you don't locate anything today?"

His thin face shadowed. "I hardly think one more day will tell the full story."

"I wish we'd never come here."

He frowned at her. "After seeing you run out after that Barnabas last night, I'm beginning to wish the same thing. What does he mean to you?"

"He's a good friend."

"You know his reputation," her father warned her. "I've heard the gossip. I don't believe all of it."

"I've always been able to reason with you," Claude Bliss said with a deep sigh. "But I seem to get nowhere when I try to make you see him in his true light."

"Because I think you're wrong," she said.

Jim Donovan came up to them and told her father, "We're ready to lower the bathysphere now, sir."

"Fine," her father said. "I'll be there in a minute." He turned to her. "Keep the communication lines clear. It's important. All of us below are dependent on you."

"I will," she said. "Take care."

He smiled and kissed her tenderly on the cheek. "This is less dangerous than the average taxi ride." And he left her to go to the stern of the tug and slide down into the circular opening of the diving bell.

Norah went to watch. In spite of what her father said there was always danger in this type of undersea exploration. It needed only some vital link to go wrong to place the men inside the sphere in immediate danger. A bad failure of power or air could wipe out their lives in a short time. She watched as the cover of the diving bell was set in place and fastened down. Then Donovan supervised the immersion of the bathysphere.

It went down quickly and when it had reached a point next to the wreck the young captain turned the telephone linked with the sphere over to her. She sat ready to take notes or pass on any urgent message to Jim Donovan.

After a moment she heard her father's voice from down on the floor of the cove, "We're beside *The Jenny Swift* and I'm studying the hull from the observation window while Clary and Mitchell prepare to go into the escape chamber and proceed to the wreck directly."

"Can you see more than the other day?" she asked.

"Yes," her father replied after a moment. "Much more clearly. There is no question that the side of the vessel has a large opening cut in it. I would say major salvage has been carried on here."

"Are the radio links with the divers operative?" Norah wanted to know.

"Yes," her father said. "Using our special new equipment they'll be able to report to me directly as they make their way around inside the wreck."

Captain Donovan came to her. "I have some information regarding the tide and currents," he said. "I'd better give it personally to your father."

She smiled and passed the telephone to him. "It is all yours, Captain."

She was glad to have a few minutes free from the responsibility of keeping contact with the sphere. She was nervous all the time. Afraid her father might send up some urgent message for help. She'd not yet come to trust the new addition to their salvage equipment.

Her mind filled with these thoughts, she walked to the other end of the tug and stood there staring at the shore. The cliffs stood high along this part of the coast and she could clearly see Carson Blythe's modern mansion on the cliff face and the contrasting Gothic mansion of Collinwood dominating its own area.

"An interesting sight, isn't it?" a pleasant voice beside her said. And she turned to see David Cartill standing there dressed in the rough clothes of the crew. There was a mocking smile on his goateed face.

CHAPTER 11

Norah was both enraged and surprised. She couldn't imagine the young man having enough gall to smuggle himself aboard the salvage boat. But here he was disguised as one of the crew and enjoying himself.

She said, "What nerve you have!"

"Because I'm here?" He chuckled. "I think it's the best possible place to protect the interests of myself and my wife. I can follow exactly what you do about the treasure."

"You have no rights," she said angrily. "You may still fool the others, but I know you're an impostor!"

He stared at her. "How could you know?"

"I've been warned about you, Quentin Collins," she said angrily. "And I'm going to tell the captain you're on board."

"You don't want him to make a special trip ashore on my account," he protested.

"We can send you back in a rowboat," she said. "That's hardly being hospitable," the young man said, his eyes twinkling.

"Why should we be hospitable to you?" she demanded. "You've done nothing but threaten and cause trouble. And you condemned Barnabas wrongly."

He nodded wisely. "Now I think I know why you're so against me. You're devoted to Barnabas."

"He's my friend."

"And so I automatically must be your enemy? I don't think that's very logical."

"You lied about Barnabas attacking your wife. You haven't even got a wife. You're a pathological liar and troublemaker!"

"Dear! Dear!" he said. "I don't think even Barnabas would speak of me so harshly."

She sighed and stared at him with despair. "What else can I say? You're impossible! Completely without conscience!"

He smiled happily, his wavy hair blowing in the breeze. "I wish that were true. But unfortunately I am burdened with one."

"It must be very tiny then," she said. "When I think of you running wildly in that cemetery last night and injuring Dr. Hoffman."

"I did that?" He looked startled. "You're badly in error."

She studied him with resignation. "Barnabas said you wouldn't be able to remember anything about it."

"At least he was right in that," the young man said. "And now let us look at some facts. Barnabas isn't above reproach either. He is not a bright shining star with the Collins family."

"They are unfair to him."

"And why can't they also be said to be unfair to me?"

"Ah," she said. "So you do admit to being Quentin?"

The blond man looked smug. "I don't admit to anything."

"I could have you put off this tug right away," she warned him.

His twinkling eyes met hers again. "But you won't."

"Don't be too sure."

"Not even if I promise to be on my best behavior?"

"Is that possible?"

"Word of honor," he said.

Norah found herself amused by his nerve in spite of herself. And she had an idea he did mean to keep his promise. Barnabas had carefully pointed out that Quentin was more reckless and mischievous than wicked. Perhaps she should give him a test.

"Very well," she said. "I'll trust you. I'm going back to my post on the underwater phone. I'll depend on you to behave."

He gave her one of his winning smiles. "I'll keep my word."

She left him there and went back to the stern end of the tug. Jim Donovan was waiting for her. As he turned the phone over to her again, he said, "Who were you talking to up there? I don't recognize him as one of the crew."

"He's not," she said. "He's a gate-crasher."

The young captain showed annoyance. "So we're going to be bothered with some of them."

"Don't do anything about him," she said.

"You're sure?" Jim Donovan showed surprise.

"Yes. He's a sort of friend of mine. I don't think he'll get in your way."

"It's up to you, Miss Bliss," the Captain said.

She sat down at the phone again for a vigil that would go on to the end of the day. She could hear her father exchanging conversations with the divers and every so often he would speak over the line extending up to her.

Around two in the afternoon he came through with a message, saying, "We've just found a small chest. Clary is bringing it back to the diving bell. Maybe this is the beginning of a real find. He hasn't been able to locate anything else."

"Let's hope the chest is loaded with diamonds," she said from the deck end of the telephone.

Her father chuckled. "It's about our only hope, it seems."

"How much longer will you be down there today?" she asked.

"We'll see after we get the chest safely in here," her father said. "It's bright down here now. We'll work as long as possible."

Not until five-thirty did they bring the diving bell back to the surface of the cove. Norah felt relieved as she saw the top removed from it and her father emerge to be helped up onto the deck.

The first thing she asked him was, "Did you open the chest yet?"

"No," he said. "It's badly corroded and rusted. I waited until we could work at it here on the deck."

"I'm excited," she confessed.

"I won't deny I am," her father said with a smile on his weary, lined face. And he turned to watch the two divers come up onto the deck with the chest.

Norah stood over it filled with the excitement she always knew when they came upon these secrets of the ocean depths. The chest was indeed small; even if it were filled with golden sovereigns the treasure wouldn't amount to much. It had to be diamonds or other precious jewelry. And Clary said that it wasn't very heavy.

They cut through the rusted iron lock and some of the heavy iron ribs of the chest with a hacksaw, then inserted a small crow bar to force it open. In a moment it gave way with a protesting squeak.

She stared into the chest and then gave a gasp of disappointment. All it contained were faded silks and laces which had been ruined by their long immersion in the salt water. There was no gold! No diamonds!

Clary, on his knees before the chest, disgustedly threw the contents on the deck. He looked up at her father apologetically. "Sorry, Chief!"

Her father seemed to have aged in a few minutes. He stared at the empty chest and the sorry contents which had been strewn out beside it. "Not your fault, Clary. You brought something back."

"The ship has been stripped," the diver complained.

"So it seems. What about the after-hold?"

"It's the only section we haven't completely gone through," Clary said. "We can get at it tomorrow. But I wouldn't count on anything."

"I'm not," her father said and turned away from the chest to lean on the railing of the tug and stare at the ocean.

She came and stood beside him. "It's a shame, Dad!"

He gave her a rueful smile. "You can't always win."

"It seems there's just nothing down there!"

Her father sighed. "Perhaps tomorrow."

"I wish you'd give up and leave," she begged him. "I don't think our luck will change. There may be something in that curse."

Her father looked sad. "I hardly expected you to say that."

"It could be."

"I'll work until the end of the week," her parent said. "If we find nothing by then I'll call it quits."

"A week seems such a long while," she worried.

"It's not a complete week and the time will pass quickly enough," he said. And he turned to go to the small cabin. As he did he almost bumped into the young man with the blond goatee.

David Cartill said, "Not much to quarrel over in today's catch."

Her father glared at him. "What are you doing on board?"

The young man shrugged. "It was a nice day and I was interested."

Claude Bliss looked as if he might have a stroke. He pointed an angry finger at him. "Let me tell you, young man, this is my boat. And you were not invited aboard. I should have them toss you over the side!"

Norah touched her father's arm. "Wait, Dad. I could have sent him back to shore. But he promised to cause no trouble if I allowed him to stay. So I gave him permission and he's behaved very well."

Astounded, her parent gasped, "He's your guest?"

She smiled. "In a way. Please let it go at that"

"Thanks, Norah," the young man said.

Her father took a deep breath. "Very well, young man, you'll not be bothered this time. But if I ever discover you aboard again, count on swimming to shore!"

"Yes, sir," the young man said and he had the good sense to move on.

Her father went down into his cabin and remained there until the tug reached the wharf. When they climbed off the tug, Norah missed the young man. There were a number of people on the wharf and he somehow got off without their seeing each other.

When she and her father walked up the wharf they came face to face with Carson Blythe and his foster daughter, who had been standing there watching the tug land.

Carson Blythe asked her father, "Any better luck today, Mr.

Bliss?"

"I'm afraid not," he said.

The millionaire looked grim. "I warned you."

"I'd like to talk to you about your salvage attempts," her father said. "Can I drop by your place this evening?"

"Grace and I would be delighted to have you and your daughter visit us again," Carson Blythe said.

"No. I'd prefer this to be a business talk between us two," her father suggested. "We can have the ladies with us another time."

The millionaire shrugged. "Just as you say."

"And would it be possible to contact the captain of your salvage crew?" her father asked.

Carson Blythe seemed grimly amused. "It is possible, perhaps, but doubtful. You would have to contact a competent spiritualist. Our captain died a few months after the salvage attempt failed."

"I didn't know," her father said awkwardly. "Then I'll see you at your place tonight."

"I'll expect you," Carson Blythe said. Grace had remained quiet during all the exchange. Now she offered them a nervous smile as they left.

When they were a distance away Claude Bliss said, "That daughter of his is pretty but strange."

"She seems very nervous," Norah agreed. "But then having her foster mother commit suicide was undoubtedly shocking to her. And she also has been tormented by the ghost of Jenny Swift."

"Each time you mention that ghost you sound more like someone who believes in it," her father reproached her.

She made no reply and they climbed the steep path to the lawn above. Things were tranquil at Collinwood. Not until Norah had changed into a dress for dinner and gone down to join the others was there any excitement. Her father was the center of attention when she went into the living room.

Seeing her, he left the others to come across the room and greet her. "I have some interesting information for you," he said with irony.

"What sort of information?"

Her father glanced back at Roger and the others. "I don't think she's going to like this," he said. And turning to her again, he told her, "I've had follow-up information on the Cartills from my lawyer. The real Cartills are in London at this very moment!"

"In London!"

"Yes," her father said with a triumphant smile. "And that means our Mr. Cartill and his wife are fakers!"

"But why?"

Roger Collins came up to her with one of his stem smiles. "We've come to the conclusion that the fake Cartill is our cousin Quentin. He comes back every so often, pretending to be someone else. He enjoys tormenting us."

"Have you checked with him at the cottage?" she wanted to know.

"No," Roger said. "I've done better. I've asked the police to arrest him and his wife on charges of impersonation. We'll see how that turns out!"

She couldn't help feeling a bit sorry for the young man. "Was that necessary?"

"Yes," Roger said. "He was attempting to swindle us." All through dinner she kept wondering how it would turn out. She wasn't sure that she wanted Quentin to be arrested; in many ways he could be a charming young man. And he'd done them little real harm.

When they were talking in the living room after dinner, the state police arrived to speak privately with Roger Collins.

While they awaited Roger's return to the living room, Norah's father checked his wristwatch and said, "I soon must leave for Blythe's."

"You're sure you don't want me to go with you?" she asked.

"No," he said, very seriously. "I think I may be able to get more sense out of him if I see him strictly alone."

"Maybe you're right," she said. "But I think Grace is lonesome. Tell her I'd enjoy having her come here some evening."

"I'll invite them both," her father said. "I'm sure Elizabeth won't mind." Elizabeth and Carolyn had gone upstairs.

Roger came back into the room frowning after the state police left. He gave a disgusted sigh. "The same old story!"

Norah asked, "What is it?"

"By the time the police reached the cottage, both Quentin and that girl with him had left. And no one could say where they'd gone."

"I'm not surprised," her father said.

"He knows now the treasure hunt is probably going to be a failure." Roger said, "Besides which, he has a healthy dislike for prisons. I suppose we may as well wish him good luck until the next time. He'll show up again one day, count on it."

"He was a strange person," she said. "In some ways I like him."

"That's always been true." Roger surprised her by admitting this. "But I still see him as a scoundrel. With him gone there's only Barnabas left."

"You can't think of him and Barnabas in the same light?" she said, amazed.

Roger looked at her coldly. "Why not? They've both done a lot to tarnish the family name."

"I can't see Barnabas doing anything to shame you."

"I'm glad you still have a few illusions concerning him," Roger said with some sarcasm. "I'm afraid I haven't" Roger went on to the study and her father left for his visit with Carson Blythe. She waited alone in the living room, hoping that Barnabas might appear. She wanted to tell him about Quentin. But the time passed and Barnabas did not show up.

She knew there were some nights when he didn't visit Collinwood, but he had promised her to stay in touch with her. She felt only something very serious could have prevented him keeping his word. When it was almost midnight she gave up. He had warned her to be patient. This was truly a test of her.

She went upstairs to her bedroom. She supposed Carolyn and her mother were long asleep. Her father hadn't returned, but perhaps he had finally succeeded in getting Blythe to talk seriously about his salvage hunt. That could keep him very late.

She locked the doors as usual. But she did not leave the bathroom light on. She wasn't all that nervous. Somehow she felt things were changing at the old mansion; maybe much of the danger had passed. After a long vigil of staring up into the dark shadows of the room she finally fell asleep.

Again her sleep was tormented with dreams of Jenny Swift. The lithe figure of the pirate captain appeared in all her nightmares. Norah somehow felt she was on the ancient pirate vessel with the beautiful but ruthless pirate queen. She watched as Jenny subdued a mutinous and motley crew. The titian beauty used her long blacksnake whip with devastating effect. And then she turned to smile at Norah but she turned too far and that horribly mutilated face was revealed. Norah screamed!

Norah tossed restlessly beneath the light covering on her bed. Again she was on the deck of *The Jenny Swift* and the pirate queen after whom the ship was named had several prisoners with their hands tied behind their backs lined up before her. An evil henchman with a black patch over his eye and a musket in his hands roamed up and down the line making sure the prisoners behaved.

Norah studied their faces and was shocked to discover Roger, Barnabas, Captain Jim Donovan and her father among the bound captives. Jenny smiled cruelly at her prisoners and then told her henchman to bring one of them a few feet forward. The man with the black patch brought her father stumbling forward. He stood there staring straight ahead, his thin face the picture of dignity.

"Father!" she cried out to him. But he gave no hint of hearing her.

Jenny Swift laughed and then lifted the whip high so that its cruel rippling black lash curled through the air. And with expertise she brought it down so the lash wrapped itself around the throat of Norah's father. She heard his groan and saw him drop to the deck.

The pirate queen withdrew the whip and left him stretched out there. She nodded to the henchman with the black eye patch to produce another victim. This time it was Jim Donovan who was shoved roughly in front of her.

"Please!" Norah begged for Jim.

The pirate queen ignored her, raising the whip again. This time she let it wrap around the young captain's chest. A spasm of pain twisted his good-looking face and he staggered, but did not collapse. Jenny Swift withdrew the lash and then swung it hard against him once again. He slumped to his knees to collapse face forward on the deck.

"Let him be!" Norah screamed. And she was still screaming when she woke to the darkness of the room.

The feeling of horror which had invaded her sleep remained with her now that she was awake. A sense of great danger made her rise up in the bed and stare into the shadows. She was sure she was not alone. And then very slowly the phantom took shape. Jenny Swift!

"No!" Norah whispered hoarsely.

But the ghost of the pirate queen grew more distinct each second. Now the phantom was beside her bed and the beautiful profile was swiftly turned so the battered, mutilated one was revealed. The obscenity of that eye hanging from the socket over the sunken cheek was too much! Norah had undergone too many torments to be able to add this one. Mercifully she fainted.

When she came to, she knew at once the thing had gone. She was alone. Though she was still fearful, she managed to turn on her bedside lamp and there was no sign of anyone in the room. Then her eyes automatically moved to her bedspread. The wet strands of seaweed from the phantom's hair were there. She drew back in revulsion from them.

It was near dawn and she slept no more that night. When daylight came she forced herself to clean the seaweed from her bed and dispose of it. By the time Lucy came with her breakfast tray she was dressed.

Lucy seemed in a good mood as she remarked, "We're promised fine weather for today, miss."

"I'm glad," she said.

"Will you be going out on the tug again?"

"Yes," she said. "I work with my father."

"Master David claims he's going along one day," the stout girl said. "I don't think he should. Not with that curse and all."

Norah was seated at the tray. "You believe in the curse, don't you?"

"Yes, miss."

"And Jenny Swift's ghost?"

"Indeed I do, miss," the stout girl said. "Too many have seen it to deny it. And then look what it did to Mr. Blythe and his wife."

"I suppose you have good grounds for your fears," Norah admitted.

"Live here along this lonely coast long and you'll understand," the girl told her. And she went on out.

Norah dallied over her breakfast. She was in a strange mood, a mood she couldn't quite understand. One thing she did recognize: she must confide her experiences to her father. It was time he knew the true horror of the pirate queen's curse. That she had been the victim of several visitations already. How long could she stand it? How many more nights before her nerves would break? Then she'd take the same route of self-destruction as Carson Blythe's wife!

She finished her coffee and decided to go downstairs. In the hallway she met Roger Collins, who looked worried.

"I'm glad you've come down," he said.

"Oh?"

"Your father hasn't shown up for breakfast," Roger explained. "And he's always down before this."

She felt herself stiffen. "Perhaps he overslept?" she suggested in a strained voice.

"No," Roger Collins said. "I've already had someone check his room. His bed hasn't been slept in. He apparently didn't return here after he went out last night."

She felt she might faint. Roger Collins must have seen her waver for he came to her aid quickly, grasping her by the arm and supporting her. "There's probably nothing to worry about," he said quickly. "He must have stayed so late at Blythe's he decided to remain there all night."

Her eyes had glazed over. "Find out," she said in a weak voice that sounded far away and unlike her own.

"I will," Roger assured her. "I was just going to make the phone call. Let me find you a chair first." And he guided her into the living room and an easy chair.

"Hurry, please!" she begged him.

"Don't panic," he said placatingly. "I'm sure there's nothing to be concerned about. I'll make the phone call right here in the hall. You wait there."

"Ask them," she said, dully, so deep in shock she hardly knew what she was saying.

Then she heard Roger Collins on the line, his tone casual and businesslike at first. Then there was some surprise in his voice and he stammered a little. There was another short pause and when he spoke the next time he had lost all his authority. His tone was one of stunned despair. She heard him put the phone down and his footsteps as he walked across the hardwood floor to her.

She didn't yet dare raise her eyes to look at his face. She knew it would be a mask of dismay. She heard him say, "I don't understand! I simply don't understand!"

"What did they tell you?"

"Your father left Carson Blythe's fairly early. But when they checked the parking lot just now they saw that his car is still there. They can't imagine why unless he decided to walk back home along the beach and stop by the wharf to see some of the crew who live on the barge."

"Have you talked to Captain Donovan?" she managed.

"No. We'll do that next," Roger Collins said more calmly. "He must have stopped by the tug and stayed there all night."

"Why?" she asked hopelessly.

"I don't know," Roger admitted. "Perhaps after the conversation with Carson Blythe he wanted to discuss some things with Donovan."

"Maybe."

"I'll send someone down to the wharf at once," Roger Collins said. "In the meantime, you mustn't think the worst."

He left her and she sat there almost completely oblivious to what was happening around her. She was nearly certain her father had come to some dreadful end. Last night's dream had offered a certain dread symbolism. The curse had surely struck again. Meanwhile she awaited word from the wharf, even though she didn't expect it to offer her any comfort.

Elizabeth came by and said, "You poor dear girl!"

Norah was beyond the polite gesture of thanking her. Then Carolyn hovered close only to vanish. Obviously the entire household was shocked by what had happened; Norah couldn't help wondering if they were all as despairing as she concerning her father's fate.

Roger impinged on her consciousness again. He was bending close to her. "I have no good news," he said sadly. "He didn't show up at the wharf. No one there has seen him."

"I knew it would be that way," she murmured.

Roger stared at her. "Where do you think he is?"

At last she looked up at him. "I think he's dead," she said simply.

"No!" he protested, horror crossing his stern face. "We mustn't think anything like that."

But she knew. And so she waited. Finally Jim Donovan came to her with the word about her father.

Standing awkwardly before her, he said, "On the beach. His body was washed up on the beach a few minutes ago."

Her head bowed. "I knew it."

"They think he must have been walking back and had a heart attack." The young captain faltered. "There's just one thing."

"Yes?" she raised questioning, terrified eyes to meet his solemn ones.

"It's his neck," Donovan said. "There's a welt mark around his neck like the lash of a whip!"

CHAPTER 12

In that moment she was finally convinced of the reality of the curse and the phantom Jenny Swift. And not even when the official coroner later gave a report of her father's death as from simple heart failure minimizing the cruel red line around his throat as a scratch of unknown origin, did she change her opinion. Her father had died under the ghostly whip of Jenny Swift. It had to be!

Of course everyone was very kind to her. The Collins family did not appear to think it strange when she requested that her father's body be cremated and his ashes scattered on the waves at the site of his last salvage operation. Barnabas had requested that she defer the ceremony until dusk so that he might be there with her.

So one evening more than a week after her father's death the tug moved out into the cove with a group of those associated with the venture on board. There were special invited guests such as Carson Blythe and his foster daughter, who had been especially thoughtful of her during this period of tragedy, and a few others including Barnabas, Dr.Hoffman and Professor Stokes.

Roger Collins stood stern-faced as Norah, assisted by Barnabas, scattered the ashes over the water. It was dark when the simple ceremony ended and they returned to the wharf. A gathering of the backers of the salvage operation followed in the living room of Collinwood.

Julia Hoffman began the discussion by asking Norah, "Do you intend to spend any more time investigating the wreck of *The Jenny Swift*?"

Norah had given this a great deal of thought. Now she said, "Yes. I would like to send Clary down to finish checking the after hold. If he finds nothing there the mission has failed."

Roger Collins, standing by the fireplace, gave her a searching glance. "Are you sure it is worth going to this extra trouble? None of us would blame you for abandoning the project."

"Please believe that," Elizabeth Stoddard chimed in. From the chair in which she was sitting, Norah studied them all. She knew they were all anxious to do their best for her. But she had to carry this out according to her own judgment.

She said, "I think we should finish what we have started."

"A good principle," the professor agreed.

Dr. Hoffman looked worried. "As long as it means no danger for Norah," she said.

Elizabeth nodded. "That is something to consider."

Norah smiled bitterly. "Of course you're thinking about the curse. Just tonight after the ceremony Carson Blythe came to me and warned me again."

"He does feel very strongly about it," Julia Hoffman said. "But then that is natural, since he suffered from it so much himself."

"I understand that," Norah said. "And I'm aware of the danger. But I do want to finish what my father began. I think it is what he would want."

Barnabas, who had been silent up to this point, said, "In that case you should proceed."

Roger Collins cleared his throat "Very well. We'll expect you to resume and settle the business within a few days."

With that the official discussion of the project ended, but there was some general conversation before the group broke up. Norah found herself talking to Professor Stokes while from the corner of her eye she watched Barnabas and Julia Hoffman in earnest conversation a distance away.

Professor Stokes asked her, "When you finish here will you continue operating the salvage company?"

"Only if I can find a suitable manager," she said. "So many phases of it require a man's hand."

The stout man showed interest. "What about Captain Donovan? He appears to be very competent."

"He could be a possibility."

"I'd think he'd be the ideal man," the professor said. "He is familiar with your father's methods and you know him well as a person."

"We'll probably discuss it later," she said. She'd not recovered enough from the shock of everything to turn to a consideration of the future. But this would soon be necessary.

Professor Stokes glanced over at Barnabas and said, "You seem to get along very well with the British cousin."

"Barnabas and I are good friends," she said quietly.

Professor Stokes looked solemn. "It is a pity Dr. Hoffman wasn't able to be of more help to him. Though it is perhaps largely his own fault. He didn't give her a proper chance to complete his treatments."

"Do you think he'll ever return to the hospital?"

"I doubt it," Professor Stokes said. "He will probably soon be moving on. He is a true wanderer."

Julia had finished her conversation with Barnabas and now she came over to them with a smile. She told the Professor, "We have to be going." And to Norah she said, "I've just been telling Barnabas I'm worried about you."

"I'll manage," she said quietly.

"I hope so," the doctor said. "If you need me, if there's anything I can do, please get in touch with me."

"Thanks," she said. "I'll remember that."

She and Barnabas saw Dr. Hoffman and the professor to their car. Afterward they walked hand in hand through the starry spring night. The first hint of warmer weather had come to the bleak Maine area.

She glanced at Barnabas as they strolled along the cliff path in the direction of Widows' Hill. "You are very silent tonight."

"It has been a sad evening," he said.

"In a way," she agreed. "But not as bad for me as the time when I first heard that father was dead."

"Then you've adjusted," Barnabas said.

"As well as I can."

"You should try and wind things up here as quickly as possible," he told her.

She gave him a searching look. "You'd have been happier if I'd decided not to stay."

"Yec."

"Why?"

"For various reasons."

They had come to the high point of the cliffs known as Widows' Hill and they halted there. She turned to look up into his gaunt, handsome face. "You believe as I do that my father died from the curse."

"I haven't said so."

"You don't have to. I can tell."

He frowned. "If you also believe it, why do you insist on finishing what is obviously going to be a failed operation?"

Her eyes met his. "Because I want to defy her!"

"The phantom?"

"Yes. I want to challenge her. Maybe I'm silly enough to think I can somehow set her avenging spirit to rest for all time."

"Others have tried that without success," Barnabas reminded her.

"This will be my try. I owe it to father."

"You don't owe him anything. All he would want is your safety, you must know that."

"I'm no longer so concerned with my own safety," she said. "I want to end her reign of terror over this place."

His eyes were filled with concern. "I will soon be leaving here. And I don't want to go before you do."

"Why must you leave?"

"You surely are aware that I'm no longer welcome," Barnabas said in a bitter voice. "Roger has already spoken to me on the quiet. It seems the villagers resent and fear me."

"They're being unfair."

"I'm used to that," Barnabas said. "So, like Quentin, I must soon take my leave."

"Quentin!" she said with grim resignation. "He helped confuse things with his tricks. I wonder where he is now?"

Barnabas smiled thinly. "He could be nearer here than you think. At any rate he always comes back sooner or later."

"And so do you."

"The place has a hold on us," Barnabas said. "Even the renegades of the family have a longing to return here occasionally."

"You're no renegade," she said softly.

"Don't be too sure."

"Barnabas, I need a man to help me run the salvage company. You would be wonderful for it. Why don't you marry me and we'll roam the world just as you're doing now. I'll make a good wife and I'll never interfere with your wishes."

He smiled at her gently. "What a wonderful offer."

"I mean it," she said with great earnestness.

"I wish it were possible," Barnabas said.

"Only you are standing in the way of our happiness."

"I know," he sighed. And he drew her close to him for a lasting kiss. When he let her go, he said, "You say you are deliberately challenging the phantom."

"Must we talk about that now?"

"Yes. I have only a few minutes more."

"Well?"

"You are convinced the ghost killed your father, just as Carson Blythe insists his wife was a similar victim?"

"True."

"And you have seen the ghost."

"I have."

"On the grounds and then in your bedroom."

"Several times in my bedroom," she agreed. "At first I thought it was part of a nightmare, but the seaweed on my bed ended that."

Barnabas wore a strained expression. "Collinwood is a strange place. I know it better than most people. And yet it has secrets from me. Why don't you ask Elizabeth to change your room?"

"After my being in it this long while? She'd think it odd."

"No matter."

"And besides, I don't want to move. If the phantom is truly coming to threaten me again I want to be there to face her."

"Part of your challenge?" he asked wryly.

"You could call it that."

"So you won't take my advice?"

"No. Not this time."

He stared at her with resignation. "That doesn't leave me much choice."

"Choice about what?"

"About how I'm to help you," he said.

Her eyes met his probingly. "You could help me most by becoming my husband, Barnabas."

His smile was bitter. "It's time to take you home."

He walked her back to the ancient mansion and kissed her goodnight. She went inside with a feeling of depression and loneliness. In spite of everything she could only get so close to Barnabas and then he eluded her. She was beginning to despair that they would ever have a future together.

Standing in the shadowed entrance hall she gazed up at the portrait of his ancestor which hung there and looked so much like him. With a sigh, she spoke to the painting aloud. "He is just as inscrutable as you must have been." And she turned and started up the shadowed stairway.

The following morning the salvage operation was resumed. Norah found herself with more responsibility now, though Jim Donovan was very helpful. She was beginning to weigh Professor Stokes' words very carefully and wonder if he wouldn't be the ideal person to continue the business with her.

They stood together in the bow of the tug as it moved out

into the cove. Turning to him, she said, "What are your plans when we finish here?"

He gave her a surprised glance. "I haven't made any."

"There is a possibility I may wind up the business," she warned him.

He looked unhappy. "I hope not. The crew aren't expecting it."

She smiled incredulously. "Do they actually think I'll carry on alone?"

His young, pleasant face was earnest. "We all have a great deal of loyalty to you and the business, Miss Bliss."

"We know each other well enough for you to call me Norah."

He smiled. "I didn't want to take any liberties."

"You're not the type to do that, Jim," she told him. "And if you and the crew have so much faith in me perhaps I'd better think about continuing on."

"I would, Norah," he said, saying her name so shyly it amused her.

They arrived at the scene of the salvage operation and then the serious work of the day began. Norah lost herself in the busy routine and excitement of the underwater exploration. She went down in the diving bell with Clary and Mitchell, and supervised their investigations over the radio telephone as her father had.

It was another world down there. Small schools of fish swam by her wide observation window; she could study the encrusted hull of *The Jenny Swift* and watch the progress of the divers as they moved like sleepwalkers along the ocean floor, pressing the tall underwater growth to one side when it was in their way.

From the after hold the voice of Clary came over the phone, "It's no different here from the rest of the ship. Miss Bliss. A passage has been cut through to the other section and whatever of value was down here has been removed."

"You're certain?" she asked.

"Certain." He was emphatic.

"Then we may as well call it quits," she told him. And she at once called the other diver in.

It was late afternoon before she emerged from the diving bell to the deck of the tug and told Donovan, "There's no treasure down there. Nothing. We're winding up here and saving our energies and capital for the next operation."

He smiled at her. "I say that's wise just so long as there's going to be another operation."

"There will be," she said. "I've decided that."

They headed the tug back to the wharf. She was relieved but

more than a little angry. She had paid the price of being tormented by the ghost of Jenny Swift and gained none of the benefits. It didn't seem fair. And even though she'd given up the underwater exploration she wasn't finished with the affair. What she had still to do could be accomplished on land.

It did not surprise her that Carson Blythe and his foster daughter, Grace, were waiting on the wharf for her return. She knew the morbid interest he had in the salvage venture, and she felt a deep sympathy for him. He had lost his wife just as she had lost her father, and neither of them had brought back any of the treasure. It made a real bond between them.

When she stepped onto the wharf he came over to her. "How did it go today?"

She shrugged. "I'm convinced now there is nothing there."

"I disagree with you in that," Carson Blythe said solemnly. "I think all the treasure is down there someplace. But the ghost of Jenny Swift is jealously guarding it. No human will ever salvage the gold and precious jewels."

She stared at him. "You honestly think that?"

"Yes."

"You could be right. I'm not prepared to argue. I have another theory. And I'm going to begin at once trying to prove it." .

Grace looked interested. "Another theory?"

"Yes," Norah said. "I'm positive that one of the other salvage expeditions found the treasure and kept it a secret. That *The Jenny Swift* was stripped bare some years ago. I'm going to trace back those various ventures and check them out until I find who did get the treasure."

"That's a fantastic idea," Grace exclaimed.

Her foster father showed irritation. "You'll get nowhere," he predicted. "My advice is to leave here and forget all about this."

"I'm afraid I can't do that," she said quietly. "This venture cost my father his life."

The white-haired man said, "Well, at least I've tried to warn you."

Grace looked concerned. "Please don't leave without paying us another visit," she said.

"I'll try," Norah promised, but she doubted that she would. Carson Blythe depressed her. He was too resigned to what the phantom Jenny Swift had done to him.

After dinner that evening she told Roger Collins and his sister, Elizabeth, of her decision. "I'm not giving up on the treasure hunt," she explained, "I'm going about it in a different way."

Roger Collins was extremely interested. "Will you be able to get a complete list of the various salvage operations?"

"I'm sure I can," she said. "I'll talk to the town clerk in Collinsport tomorrow. Then I may have to go on to Augusta and go through the state records."

"You're very thorough," Elizabeth marveled.

She smiled bitterly. "My father taught me that. There can be no leaving to chance or guesswork in underwater exploration."

"You'll soon be leaving us then?" Roger said.

"I've imposed too long."

"Not at all," he said. "You're still very welcome here. And come back any time you like."

"I'll remember," she said. "It may be that my investigation will bring me here again. I don't know."

"It's been a most interesting experience," Roger Collins said. "Nothing like this has ever happened at Collinwood before."

The evening progressed and she waited to see Barnabas. Again she planned to ask him to let her share his life. But he disappointed her by not showing up at Collinwood. By the time she realized he wasn't coming, it was too late to go in search of him. So instead she went up to bed.

She'd no sooner reached her bedroom than she heard a car pull up in the driveway in front of the old mansion. She knew it must be Carolyn returning from her date for the evening. She heard Carolyn get out of the car and say goodnight; then the front door opened and closed and there were the sound of footsteps on the stairs.

After the car drove off there was silence again. Norah changed into her night dress and got into bed. This could be her last night at Collinwood and it gave her a strange, tense feeling. So much had happened since she'd arrived there with her father. Now she would be leaving alone ... unless Barnabas changed his mind and joined her.

Her head on the pillow, she stared up at the darkness. What about the ghost of Jenny Swift? Would it follow her when she left Collinwood? She was still debating it when she fell asleep.

When the rustling sound made its way through to her she opened her eyes and sat up quickly. It was still dark but she suddenly realized that she was not alone in the room. Her first thought was that the phantom had come again. She had challenged Jenny Swift and the female pirate was not one to avoid such defiance.

Staring into the shadows, her heart beating rapidly, she saw the familiar form of the phantom Jenny take shape. The ghost moved slowly across the room towards her. But there was a difference! This time the phantom carried the long blacksnake whip in her hand.

Norah screamed and at the same time the whip lashed through the air to curl around her like a stinging snake. It took Norah's breath away. Before she could recover, the whip came at her again and she had a glimpse of that horrible mutilated face just above her. She fell from the bed under the second impact of the lash and twisted in pain on the floor. She was vaguely aware of the whip snaking through the air ready to strike her again when something intervened.

It took her a moment to realize a third presence was in the room—and a little longer to know it was Barnabas. There was another hoarse scream but this time it was from the phantom Jenny Swift!

"The lights!" Barnabas cried.

She groped for the lamp on the bedside table and found the switch. She turned as light filled the room and saw Barnabas with the phantom in his grasp. He reached up and snatched the grotesque mask from the phantom's face to reveal the hate-distorted features of Carson Blythe!

Norah gasped. "No!"

Blythe glared at her with a madman's malevolence. "You wouldn't listen! You had to push it this far!"

Barnabas gave her a warning look. "Go downstairs and phone the state police. Tell them we have a would-be murderer here!"

She didn't wait for second instructions. The sight of the mad Carson Blythe was more than she could stand. She was content to get out of the room as quickly as she could. In the corridor she met Roger Collins who had been roused by the uproar in her room.

"What is it?" he demanded.

"In there," she said, indicating her room. "Carson Blythe." And she hurried on downstairs to call the police.

The period of waiting for the state police was a nightmare. Later they came and took a raving Carson Blythe into custody. It was clear he was destined for a hospital for the criminally insane rather than a prison. Next the police continued their investigation at Blythe's home. Norah did not go with them, but Barnabas did, and when he returned very much later he gave an account of the police findings to her and the other waiting members of the Collins family.

Standing in the center of the living room with them all grouped around him, he said, "Carson Blythe had no difficulty getting in here and threatening Norah in her room because he knew this house as well as any of us. In fact, he had learned more about its secret passages."

"But why did he do all this?" Roger demanded.

"Greed," Barnabas said. "Greed and passion. Blythe wanted to protect the treasure. He lied when he claimed the trunks he salvaged contained nothing of value. He recovered all the treasure from *The Jenny Swift* and kept it locked in an underground vault. But he made the grave error of falling in love with his foster daughter. When his wife found he was having an affair with Grace she threatened to expose him. He then built up the ghost story and murdered his wife, making it seem a suicide. By making it appear that Jenny Swift had brought on his wife's death and ruined the salvage venture he threw everyone off the track. No one suspected he had the treasure."

Norah said, "And when we arrived he decided to carry on the charade of the curse and ghost. I must say he played the role of Jenny Swift very well."

"Not quite well enough," Barnabas said dryly. "I began to suspect him fairly early in the game. Of course when you let him know you were going to keep delving into what had happened to the treasure, you gave him no alternative but to remove you."

"He made a good try," she said.

Roger Collins looked revolted by it all. "A disgusting business," he said. "Greed and passion! You are right in summing it up that way, Barnabas."

The others went up to bed and she saw Barnabas to the door. They stood alone in the shadowed hallway. "Well, it's over," she said.

"I'm glad for your sake," he told her.

"What will happen to Grace?" she worried.

"Not much. She wasn't in on the murder plots. But she was too weak to escape from his control and reveal what she suspected."

"So in a way she was an accomplice."

"In a minor way," Barnabas agreed. "I doubt if they'll be too hard on her."

She gazed up at him. "I might have known you would be the one to end all the tragedy."

He smiled wryly. "You did your part. You insisted on making yourself the bait for Blythe."

"I wanted a showdown."

"And you had one," he said. "I imagine you're satisfied, even though it nearly cost you your life."

"That's about it," she admitted.

He hesitated, then said, "I must go. It will soon be dawn."

Her eyes were gentle. "And that is the one thing you cannot face. Poor Barnabas!"

He looked startled. "You know what I am?"

Rather than answering him directly, she looked up at the

portrait hanging above them in the shadowed hall. Staring at it, she murmured, "I prefer to say I know who you are."

"You've guessed!" His voice was tense.

She looked directly at his gaunt, handsome face once more. "Yes. I've guessed. Why don't you turn to Julia Hoffman again? She loves you. And she may be able to rescue you from the vampire curse."

"I thought you wanted me to go away with you?"

She shrugged. "I know that's hopeless now. And I want what is best for you. You see I still do love you, Barnabas, even though you're beyond my reach."

He said nothing but took her in his arms. Their kiss was long and perhaps the most satisfying she'd ever known. When he slowly released her, he said, "Good luck, Norah."

She was smiling though her eyes were bright with tears. "Good luck to you, Barnabas. I'll always remember."

"I wonder," he said, staring at her with sad eyes. "You see, you know so little about time." And then he left. The last she saw of him was as he hurried off through the gray-black false dawn toward the old house.